Leslie rac

Yesterday she'
morning sickness

Was she ever wro

Leslie was slumped on the floor when she opened her eyes and saw a man's tasseled loafers. Her eyes moved upwards—suit pants, jacket, tie...furious expression.

Darn. This wasn't the way it was supposed to be when she told Hugh about the baby. She'd planned a cozy scene out by the pool, the two of them having a nightcap—his champagne, hers apple juice—she wearing something flowing and sexy.

Revealing all while doubled up on the bathroom floor in a wrinkled cotton nightshirt, her teeth unbrushed and hair a mass of tangles, was certainly not even close to her scenario.

"What's wrong? Are you overdoing it? I want some straight answers, Les."

"I'm perfectly healthy." She paused before adding, "For a pregnant woman."

Kate Denton is a pseudonym for the Texas writing team of Carolyn Hake and Jeanie Lambright. Friends as well as co-authors, they concur for the most part on politics and good Mexican restaurants, but disagree about men—tall versus short—and what constitutes good weather—sun versus showers. One thing they definitely do agree on, though, is the belief that romance in not just for the young!

Recent titles by the same author:

FIRM COMMITMENT
THE WEDDING ESCAPADE

A MARRIAGE WORTH KEEPING

BY
KATE DENTON

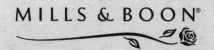

MILLS & BOON®

*MILLS & BOON and MILLS & BOON with the Rose Device
are registered trademarks of the publisher.*

*First published in Great Britain 1998
Harlequin Mills & Boon Limited,
Eton House, 18-24 Paradise Road, Richmond, Surrey, TW9 1SR*

© Kate Denton 1997

ISBN 0 263 80721 5

*Set in Times Roman 11 on 11.5pt.
02-9803-49172 C1*

*Printed and bound in Great Britain
by Mackays of Chatham PLC, Chatham*

PROLOGUE

"Grow up, Leslie!" Hugh's neck was flushed and his fists clenched. They'd begun arguing on the way home from a cocktail party and had continued through the garage, up the stairs and into the bedroom. He yanked off his tie and threw it across the mahogany valet.

"I am grown up." She kicked her sling pumps into the closet. "We had a shoestring wedding, no honeymoon—"

"By mutual agreement, remember?" His cuff links flew into the dresser caddy.

"There was a reason for it—then. But five years have passed and I want that honeymoon. I want some *quality time* with you, Hugh, not just the leavings." Her voice softened. "Paris in the spring…drinking wine in sidewalk cafés, strolling along the Seine. Please, Hugh," she cajoled, standing on tiptoe to wrap her arms around his neck.

His slow, sensuous kiss and the stubbled chin nuzzling hers made Leslie think she'd swayed him, but his words, though tenderly whispered into her ear, crushed all hope. "I want it, too," he said, sliding the zipper of her dress, baring her back for his caress. "Give me a couple of months to get through this court schedule and the trial in Houston, and—"

She jerked free. "We can't keep postponing our life together! You promised…remember?"

"I didn't promise *now*. Why do you refuse to accept my career obligations? Why do you carry on like

5

a spoiled child begrudging every second I'm away from you?" His shirt unbuttoned, he tore it off and angrily jammed it into the clothes hamper.

"Since when is it 'spoiled' to beg for a crumb of attention from one's husband? You're just name-calling to get yourself off the hook. It won't work though. I'm going to Paris. With or without you." She wriggled out of her black cocktail dress and pitched it in the direction of her closet.

"Another ultimatum?" he drawled, sitting on the bed to remove his shoes.

Leslie had issued one ultimatum after another during the last year, none of which she'd carried out. Maybe Hugh's not taking her seriously was understandable, but she had to make him see that this was no idle warning. Clad only in underwear, hands on hips, she glared down at him. "I mean it, Hugh. I'm not waiting for your schedule to clear—hell will freeze over before that happens. Like I said, I'm going with or without you!"

"Then you're damn well going alone!" he exploded. "Have a good trip." He rose and started for the bathroom.

She grabbed his arm. "If I go, I'm not coming back."

"Don't threaten me, Les. You know I have that trial—"

"There's always a trial!" She released her hold on his arm and stepped away.

"Let's not do this," he said gently, but Leslie retreated farther.

Tears were beginning to mist her brown eyes. "I don't want to, but you've given me no alternative. I feel like I've lost you."

"Don't be silly, I'm not lost. What about our plans

for the future?'' He moved closer and began stroking her cheek.

She tilted her head and his fingers stilled. ''Unless something changes, there is no future for us. Can't you see?'' Leslie's tone was pleading.

''What are you saying?''

''I'm saying our marriage isn't working.''

''All because of a delayed trip?'' he asked incredulously. ''As usual you're blowing this out of proportion.''

''It isn't just the trip. I've tried to tell you before and you haven't listened. Well now I'm going to show you. It's over.''

''Come on, Leslie, you're overreacting. If there are problems, we'll find solutions.''

''Solutions are for compatible couples. For us, there are none. There's only one way out.''

''You can't mean divorce?''

''That's exactly what I mean.''

''But we love each other.'' He paused. ''At least I love you.''

''Great way you have of showing it. When it comes to your job and me, I always rank second.''

''That's not true. For heaven's sake, Leslie, can't you see I've got a commitment here?''

She grabbed a hairbrush off her vanity and threw it at him.

Hugh deftly dodged the missile. ''Are we going to discuss this like grown-ups or do I need to find a suit of armor?''

''Discussing something like grown-ups means my acceding to your wishes. How about what *I* want for a change? How about your *commitment* to me?''

Hugh crossed the room, taking her in his arms. ''Maybe I haven't acted like it lately, but I do take that commitment very seriously. I love you, Les." He dusted her brow with a kiss.

Leslie pulled back so she could meet Hugh's eyes. "But you're still going to Houston?"

He nodded. "I don't have a choice."

She shrugged out of his arms. "Then I'm still going to Paris." She had to take a stand. It was now or never.

"Obviously you've been giving this some thought." Hugh cleared his throat and his voice seemed unsteady. "So you're intent on divorce?"

"I suppose I am."

"What will you do?"

"Travel. At first."

"Then what?"

"I don't know. I'll worry about that later."

"And our home?"

She stifled a sob. "Sell it. Auction it off to the highest bidder. Get rid of it any way you see fit."

Hugh stared at her. "You're really serious, aren't you?"

"Dead serious."

"You can't even wait a couple of days to give this some rational thought?"

"'Rational' according to you, you mean."

"No, that's not—"

"Forget it, Hugh, it's too late."

He opened his mouth as if to argue, then stopped, shaking his head sadly. "Well, if that's the way you want it, so be it. I'm sure as hell not going to get down on my knees and beg."

Suddenly both were spent and out of words, silently agreeing that there was nothing more to say. Only the whir of the digital bedside clock could be heard in the uneasy silence.

They slept in separate rooms that night and the next afternoon he caught a plane for his trial in Houston. During his absence Leslie made good her threat, packing up and leaving a note asking him to put the house on the market and initiate divorce proceedings.

CHAPTER ONE

LESLIE glared at the bedside telephone as if it were the enemy. Right now it was. Twice already she'd lifted the receiver and started to dial, then stopped. Calling Hugh was the thing she dreaded most. *But you don't have any choice.*

All it took to substantiate that thought was a glance around the small Spartan room with its generic chain-hostelry furniture. A step or so above seedy, the Resort Inn certainly offered no frills. No chocolates on the pillows, no cute little bottles of shampoo and lotions artfully arranged in the bathroom, no free cable movies on TV. And room service?—dream on. A coffee urn in the lobby and vending machines filled with stale chips and candy were it.

Not that she could afford room service. The few crumpled bills and stray coins among the pile of tissues, receipts, and gum wrappers littering her bed gave telltale signs of her grim financial status. Scarcely enough cash remained to cover take-out meals and a few more nights at this cut-rate motel. And the specter of her dwindling bank account and sky-high credit card balance made Leslie grimace. Something had to be done to prevent insolvency and it had to be done soon. That meant contacting Hugh. The house they jointly owned was her only remaining asset.

Hugh. How would he react to hearing from her? Slowly, Leslie rotated her neck, hoping to alleviate the stiffness in her body, an aftereffect of her recent illness. To no avail. She surrendered to the tiredness, the defeat, and lay down on the bed, closing her eyes. If there were any way of avoiding this encounter, she'd latch on to it in a heartbeat.

Over a year had passed since she'd left Dallas with that awful last scene ringing in her ears, the scene now embedded in her memory. Hugh had been angry, frighteningly so because he was calm—for the most part—rather than yelling and cursing. But then, she'd never seen him really lose his temper. Now that she was back, however, that's exactly what might happen.

Since the separation, Hugh had had nothing to do with her. Despite her efforts to ensure that he knew how to find her—a postcard on her arrival in France, a second two weeks later, a birthday and then a Christmas card—he'd attempted no communication. Clearly he was uninterested in her and her where-abouts.

Too distressed to rest, Leslie swung her feet to the floor and sat up, wishing she'd handled this matter earlier by mail, or better yet, retained legal counsel to speak with Hugh on her behalf. But that was the cow-ard's way out, she told herself. It was only fair to meet with him in person. More importantly, she *needed* to see him to prove that she was truly over him, that he was out of her heart. Unless she endured the acid test of being with him again, she'd never know for certain.

Once again she picked up the receiver, aggravated that her pulse was pounding in anticipation.

"Templeton, Gage and Templeton." Leslie didn't recognize the voice. The law firm must have gotten a new receptionist.

"Hugh Campbell, please."

"I'm sorry, but Mr. Campbell is no longer with us. May one of our other attorneys assist you?"

Leslie was momentarily speechless. Where was Hugh? It never occurred to her that he wouldn't be at his precious old "TGT." Had he moved away? Had something happened to him? A wave of hysteria washed over her.

"Ma'am? Are you still there?"

"Yes, I'm sorry." Leslie struggled to maintain her composure. "I must speak with Mr. Campbell personally. Do you know where I can reach him?"

"He recently started his own practice. Hold on while I locate his business card." The receptionist returned to the line and rattled off the address and a phone number.

Jotting down the information, Leslie thanked her and tried to come to grips with what this meant. Hugh'd always been career driven. After finishing law school, he'd held specific goals—recruitment by a top-notch Dallas firm as an associate, then advancing to full partner. He'd been obsessed with achieving that second objective before his thirty-fifth birthday.

From day one at TGT, Hugh's obsession had commanded his attention and energies. Long hours were put in, those hours expanding until he was leaving the house by six in the morning and often not returning until midnight. The five-day workweek stretched into six, and part of the seventh.

During his hours at home, Hugh caught up on his sleep or they made love. Eventually even sex had been sacrificed to his frenetic schedule, his all-consuming professional zeal. Either he'd be too exhausted or Leslie would rebuff him, resentful that the bedroom seemed to be the only place where he made time for her.

The sojourn in Europe, a full twelve months, had provided Leslie ample opportunity to analyze their marriage. She'd grown to regret her role in the acrimonious parting, knew she'd been hasty in leaving. But as much as she rued her rash behavior and told herself walking out the way she had was a grave tactical error, Leslie always reached the same unhappy conclusion. Even if she'd remained, the marriage was doomed. There were too many dissimilarities between them.

Hugh Campbell's world was one of order and purpose. His exquisitely tailored suits and perfectly knotted ties, his crisp white shirts and perpetually-polished shoes were a guide to the man inside. What you saw was what you got. Ambitious, upwardly mobile, Hugh structured his existence as he would a corporate planning system.

Leslie was a polar contrast. A free spirit more predisposed to T-shirts and blue jeans than to dresses and high heels, she balked at structure—at hollow traditions and meaningless rules that interfered with living life to its fullest. Her calendar was never so jammed that it squeezed out "smelling the roses."

In the beginning, Hugh had admired that *joie de vivre* just as she'd envied him his discipline and organizational skills. They'd celebrated their differences, declaring themselves two halves combining to make a whole. Yin and yang.

If they hadn't been floating on an emotional high and in a mad rush to legalize their lust, they might have recognized the fallacy in such thinking. Maybe they'd have spotted the predictable problems of two divergent personalities *before* the wedding, not years hence when it was too late. Instead of making each other miserable for five years, they could have avoided the whole unhappy experience.

Of course, they weren't always unhappy, she remembered. Sometimes.... A flashback to lazy Sunday mornings in bed, of late night skinny-dips in the backyard pool, of long lingering conversations by the fireplace. Meaningful occasions that became infrequent, finally disappearing altogether.

Leslie shook her head. What difference did it make now and why was she tormenting herself? Nothing was going to be gained by fruitless reminiscing.

As a pair, Leslie Baxter and Hugh Campbell were ill-suited under any circumstances. Total opposites falling in love too rapidly, marrying too rapidly, passion overriding common sense. Her relationship with Hugh was an unlikely union that should never have been and which of necessity was about to be relegated to the past.

As soon as you make that darn call. She resolutely dialed.

"Law offices of Hugh Campbell."

"Mr. Campbell, please."

"May I tell him your name and the nature of your call?"

These questions, and the proprietorial tone in the woman's voice, somehow ruffled Leslie and made her determined to reveal as little as possible. "It's a private matter," she answered crisply, and was met with a barely-audible sigh.

"I'm Serena Blake, Mr. Campbell's personal secretary," the woman replied, with a heavy emphasis on *personal*. "I'm afraid he's in conference right now so perhaps I can help you."

"I don't think so."

"Well, Mr. Campbell can't be disturbed at the moment. I'll have to take your name and number and have him call you." The unmistakable challenge in

the secretary's voice and her officious manner rein-
forced the streak of perverseness in Leslie.

"Fine, ask him to call Mrs. Campbell."

"His mother?"

"Oh no...his *wife*."

A pause. "His wife?"

"That's right. I can be reached at...." Leslie read
the number off.

A faint derisive huff could be heard. "I'll give him
the message, *Mrs. Campbell*," she said with exaggerated politeness. Her tone implied, "In your dreams,
lady."

"Thank you very much." Leslie banged the receiver into the cradle. Hard.

An instant later more regrets about her behavior set
in, but then Leslie's impulsive nature had been a big
problem between her and Hugh. In the beginning,
Hugh had laughed, attributing her rashness to her red-
headed temperament and calling her "my own little
will-o'-the-wisp." Later, he hadn't found her impetu-
ousness all that amusing.

With a shrug of frustration, Leslie gathered up the
money, makeup and other items cluttering the bed and
stuffed them back in the handbag. Snapping it closed,
she tossed the purse onto a chair, then lay down, her
long hair fanning over the pillow like ribbons of rust-
red silk. Despite her agitation, her eyelids began to
feel heavy. Soon her eyes closed and she fell asleep.

"So you finally decided to come home." The voice
on the phone was curt, business-like. It held none of
the warmth, the intimacy, the sensuality of the old
Hugh that had tantalized her in her dreams.

"Not exactly," she said.

"Well then, what exactly?"

Leslie eased to a sitting position and shook her head, trying to come to full wakefulness. The ringing telephone had interrupted her nap. That disruption, along with the remnants of jet lag, left her thick-tongued and disoriented. "I'd…uh…we need to discuss the house."

"What about the house?" Hugh sounded testy, almost indignant.

So much for finesse. Sixty seconds into the conversation and she'd already gotten off on the wrong foot. Leslie had planned to ease into the subject, not just blurt it out in the first minute of conversation. "I was wondering why I hadn't been notified of its sale."

"Wanting your money, huh?" he probed, giving her no opportunity to gather her wits.

"Something like that." Leslie had revived sufficiently to be irritated by his condescending, know-it-all attitude. If her survival weren't dependent on a percentage of the proceeds, she'd send this conversation into orbit right now.

"Well, that's going to be tricky. I'm sorry to disappoint you," he said, sounding anything but sorry, "but during your long excursion abroad, the real estate market's been a bummer. The 'For Sale' sign's stood in the front yard for so long, I've been expecting it to sprout roots, yet nobody's made an offer."

"Tell me you're joking."

"'Fraid not."

"There must be—"

"Look, Leslie," he interrupted, "a client is cooling his heels in the reception area. I don't have time at the moment to discuss this."

"Same old Hugh," she retorted, now wide awake. "Never enough time."

"I'm busy, Leslie," he said in a no-nonsense voice.

"If you want to talk, then come by the house tonight. That is, if your crowded travel schedule will permit. I'll be home after six."

Before she could argue or suggest an alternate site more to her liking, he'd hung up.

Her irritation rose to fever pitch. Hugh Campbell was as galling as ever. To think that she'd spent all those months in France filled with misgivings, hating herself for going off and leaving him in Dallas. What a joke! Any doubts that Hugh was too wonderful to give up should be erased by this conversation.

She'd been so apprehensive about seeing him, fearful that her old feelings might resurface. Now she began to be eager for this meeting. Being around Hugh again would be good for her, enable her to establish a mental beachhead against whimsical notions.

Following the call, Leslie soaked in a leisurely bath and silently chanted "Hugh Campbell is history." Afterward she blow-dried her hair and applied makeup—more than usual to camouflage wanness and dark shadows beneath her eyes. Hugh was not going to see her looking like death warmed over. Her plan was to march in looking as desirable as possible yet being all business.

While conducting house negotiations, she would focus on every bad thing she could remember about Hugh so that when she left, all former feelings of love and caring could be relegated to the past. Her objective was to sever all ties to him—emotional and otherwise. All she had to do was remain steadfast in that objective for another few hours. She could handle that.

Fastening the button of her silk trousers and pronouncing herself ready, Leslie recited a short affirmation as she exited from the room. She was primed.

The confidence was rudely jolted, however, by the cost of the cab ride from the Resort Inn to the house—sixteen dollars. *Will Dallas ever get decent crosstown bus service?* "There go my next three meals," she muttered under her breath while pulling out the fare for the driver.

The taxi drove away and Leslie paused at the curb, studying the home she'd shared with Hugh for three of their five married years together. A bittersweet melancholy enveloped her.

Except for new growth on the shrubs and trees, a fresh coat of paint, and that realty sign, the house looked the same—a two-story red brick with gleaming white trim and an abundance of multishaped windows. It was a lovely home and fairly priced. She'd instructed Hugh to set a figure that would guarantee a quick turnover. Why hadn't it sold?

As she moved closer to the door, Leslie's puzzlement about the house was overtaken by nervous thoughts of seeing Hugh and the fact that he wasn't answering the bell. He'd promised to be home by now. She desperately wanted to get this encounter over with and be done with him. But, if he wasn't here, she'd have to park herself on the front porch and wait.

She had no key. Along with a farewell note, she had unceremoniously dumped her keys on the hall table. A clue to show Hugh she really meant business. A gesture for her to rue, especially after a third ring of the doorbell brought no answer.

The late afternoon sun was warm and her long-sleeved blouse and lined pants better suited to air-conditioning. Perspiration was beginning to bead Leslie's forehead, her soon-to-be-ex-husband fast making her wish she'd never left the motel, much less France.

The front door finally opened and her heart was in her throat. Inches away stood the only man she'd ever loved. The sight of him sent a dozen conflicting emotions racing through her brain—and her body.

"So the prodigal's come home." Hugh was looking at her but could have as easily been addressing his remarks to a black ragamuffin dog, hardly more than a puppy, who had raced up from the adjacent yard to join Leslie at the front door. The dog apparently belonged here, his tail slapping affectionately against Hugh's pants in greeting.

"Who's this?" Leslie said, stooping to pat the pup's head.

"Man's best friend. My faithful hound Fritz." Hugh eyed the dog with mock menace. "Except when he digs under the fence to root in someone else's yard. I was out back searching for him. Fritz, meet the former mistress of the manor."

"When did you start befriending dogs? You used to say you didn't like them because they were too messy and demanding."

Hugh lifted Fritz and scratched him behind the ears. "I never said I didn't like dogs. But I'll have to admit, I was slow to recognize their true value. It's nice to have *one* relationship in my life I can depend on." As Fritz lovingly licked his face, Hugh cast a telling glance her way.

He stepped aside and motioned her into the foyer. "You indicated there was business to discuss." His voice was formal, the sniping tone gone. Hostlike, he led the way into the living room and offered her a chair. The room was exactly as it had been when she left, absent the fresh-cut flowers that she'd always had sitting on the coffee table. "I've only been home a couple of minutes and was opening a beer when I discovered Fritz missing. Can I fix you a drink? Your usual—gin and tonic?"

Leslie nodded, desirous of something cold and strong. The blueprint she'd drafted for this powwow should have included a script. Face-to-face, she could barely speak, much less ad-lib. She settled into a wing chair and watched Hugh at the bar as he added ice and a jigger of gin to a glass.

His bartending duties offered Leslie a chance to observe Hugh unnoticed. Handsome as ever, he was somehow different, his brown hair sun-streaked and longer, almost touching the top of his collar. The white shirt he wore still held its laundry starch, but his tie had been loosened and his jacket discarded, revealing Peanuts-character suspenders.

The always-formal Hugh wearing Snoopy and Woodstock—now that was an anomaly. Must have been a gift from a client, she decided. An important client.

He turned and walked toward her, bearing her drink and his beer. "And how was the Continent?" he asked, an edge to the British drawing room voice he'd affected for the question.

"You should have come along to see for yourself." Her brittle tone matched his, bite for bite.

"It's a moot point so why go into it?" Annoyance was apparent now in his voice and in the white-knuckled grip on the beer can. Bubbling right below the surface Hugh's anger was ready to spew like the tonic water from the freshly-opened bottle.

An angry Hugh was not what Leslie wanted. For the present she required his cooperation. "I agree," she soothed. "There's really no purpose in rehashing it."

His eyes appeared to glaze as he thoughtfully sipped his beer. She could tell he *was* rehashing it in his mind.

"I know this is uncomfortable for you—" she began.

"Not at all." The glaze was replaced by a scornful stare. "Are *you* uncomfortable, Leslie?"

"Perhaps *uncomfortable* was a poor choice. What I was trying to say…" She paused, groping for words. "What I was trying to say is that we might as well work out the rest of the financial details between us as expediently as possible, and get on with our lives. Since you haven't sold the house, maybe you'd be willing to buy me out."

He shook his head. "No can do."

"But why? I don't intend to hold you up on this," she said. "We can reach a fair price, something mutually advantageous."

"Fair isn't the issue, Les. I simply don't have the funds. All my spare cash is tied up in the new practice."

I need that money! Leslie wanted to cry out. Exasperated, she said, "What on earth prompted you to do such a crazy thing?"

"You mean as opposed to the prudent act of quitting your job and skipping the country?"

"Okay, okay, this is not getting us anywhere." She forced a deep breath. "Tell me about the practice," she said, hoping to calm herself. "Needless to say, I was surprised. What happened? You were so dedicated to TGT."

"For a while," he answered cryptically. "Until

large-firm politics became too much to contend with. It seemed a better idea to go out on my own.''

''And has it been a better idea?''

''Are you asking whether I'm making a decent living?'' He traced a fingertip around the rim of his can.''The bottom line was never that important to you before.''

''But it was *always* important to you,'' she countered. ''So I hope—for your sake—that it's going well.''

He rotated his hand in a ''so-so'' gesture.

''I'm not trying to pressure you, but I'm sure you can understand that I'm counting on the house sale.'' She took a sip of her drink, pleased that she'd managed to regain her composure.

His gray eyes narrowed. ''What's the problem? You left Dallas with a hefty chunk—half of our bank and savings accounts. Have you run through it already?''

Darn his hide. She slammed her glass down on the end table, sloshing some of the drink onto her pink slacks and looking down with dismay. This was her best pair! So much for composure.

Blotting the wet stain with a napkin, she raised her gaze. He might be her husband technically, but he had no right to quiz her as to why she was so low on funds. Besides, the circumstances of her current predicament were embarrassing just to think about, much less to relate to Hugh. ''What I've done with *my* money is none of your business.''

Arriving in France on a cloud of righteous indignation, Leslie'd congratulated herself on having the courage to take charge of her life. Only when the cloud vaporized did she begin to question her haste. After acknowledging the possibility of error, she'd optimistically concluded that maybe her precipitate action would bring Hugh to his senses.

She had created a fanciful scenario where he would pursue her, declare his undying love and beg her to come back to Dallas. After Hugh had demonstrated a sufficient amount of groveling, complete with promises to be a changed man, and they'd taken their holiday, she would deign to return home with him. Those were her motives for not immediately checking into work restrictions and job possibilities.

What she hadn't foreseen was complete silence from Hugh coupled with the onset of a debilitating illness. About the time she'd realized he wasn't going to come, Leslie had been diagnosed with hepatitis. She'd had to deal with the sad reality that her marriage was dead, and accept the necessity of taking her life in hand, when she was in no position to do anything. The forced bed rest and the months-long battle with poor health drained nonreplenishable dollars and prevented her from attempting to work.

Sick, in a foreign country with no friends or family around her, she'd been caught in a trap of her own making. For a variety of reasons, appealing to her family had been impossible. And if she'd phoned Dallas whining to Hugh, he'd have been skeptical, likely viewing it as a pathetic ploy to win his sympathy and lure him to her side.

After all, up to now she'd been healthy as a horse and boastful of never having as much as the sniffles. But even if he had believed her and sped to the rescue, she didn't want him back on those terms.

So let him think whatever he wished about her spending habits. At least she had a smidgen of dignity left. She shot him a disapproving glare. ''I own a share of this house—what I'm asking for is rightfully mine.''

Hugh came over with a fresh napkin to place under her glass. ''Take it easy,'' he said. ''Surely, after such a lengthy…cooling off period…we can discuss this rationally. Relax and enjoy your drink.''

He could almost hear her shriek ''Rationally! Relax!'' The Leslie Hugh remembered would have. That Leslie might even have tossed her drink at him to punctuate the words. He should know, having mopped a variety of beverages off his face during their marriage.

Too bad he couldn't burrow into that convoluted little mind of hers and figure out why she was curtailing such outbursts tonight. It rankled to think it was because of the money.

Back in his chair, Hugh settled into a lazy sprawl, relying on the feigned casualness to dispel the image of his earlier lack of discretion. That behavior had been too telling. So he'd been mad as hell when Leslie walked out. So he was still ticked off. Damned if he wanted her to know it. He could be just as composed as she about this meeting. More so.

Hugh glanced at Leslie. She'd begun nibbling her lower lip, an old nervous habit. Now he felt a surge of satisfaction. Finances might be the impetus for this meeting, but she wasn't totally impervious to him no matter how much she tried to pretend.

From the instant Serena had handed him that message slip about Leslie's call, he'd been more uptight than on a day in court before an unfriendly judge. Nice to know he wasn't the only one anxious over this reunion. ''So you want a share of the house?''

''Yes,'' she said. ''There should be some amicable way to come to terms. After all, we're two adults—''

"One and a half adults, maybe...." Hugh wanted to laugh out loud at the murderous expression in her eyes. Leslie was working so hard at suppressing her explosive nature and the effort was plainly taking its toll. *She's probably grinding a layer of enamel off her teeth right now.*

As though seeking comfort, Leslie bent to stroke Fritz's head. The traitorous dog was lying at her feet, his paws on her sandals. *Careful, pal, don't be too worshipful. She'll leave you, too,* Hugh silently warned his pet.

"Obviously, I wouldn't be here if I didn't need your assistance," Leslie said, raising her gaze to meet his again. "I want to sell the house, get my proceeds, and be on my way."

"So the house revenue goes to satisfy more of your wanderlust?" he goaded.

"That, also, is none of your business," she answered coolly.

She probably thought he'd crow if she admitted her resources had dwindled. True, he wasn't going easy on her now, but that didn't mean he wished her destitute. He'd always felt protective of Leslie, even during those times when they weren't seeing eye-to-eye.

Despite all that had happened he'd never wanted to cause her pain. Too bad she'd shown no similar concern, no contrition over the amount *she'd* inflicted.

He hunched forward, propping an elbow on the chair arm and rubbing his chin, deep in thought. "If I had any money to give you, I would, but like I said, I'm strapped for cash."

Starting up the practice had taken more capital than he'd anticipated, but a couple of lucrative cases had come his way and he'd managed to set a few dollars aside. Still he wasn't about to hand over his emergency fund to facilitate her running off again. "Wish I could help."

"Sure you do," she grumbled, indicating that she didn't believe him for a moment.

"Of course, there is a solution." He leaned back in the chair, tenting his fingers, his pose nonchalant. For moments he was silent, giving Leslie plenty of time to ponder a range of possible proposals. He felt a stab of triumph. She was going to hate his idea.

Just as he'd suspected, she snapped at the bait anyway. "And what is that solution, pray tell?"

"You could move back in."

CHAPTER TWO

HE COULDN'T be serious. Leslie tried to read his expression, but Hugh's gray eyes were impassive, his lips betraying no hint of a smile. It was a face from the past, one she'd never learned to decipher. Leslie had labeled it his "inscrutable lawyer face" and it drove her nuts. In a high-stakes poker game, that countenance would have confused a world-class card shark. Just as it was confusing her now. If this was Hugh's idea of a joke, it'd teach him a valuable lesson if she called his bluff.

"Thanks, but no thanks," she said, waiving the opportunity to score one off him. Despite her hopes of the reverse happening, the act of seeing Hugh had kindled a host of old longings. To live with him again would be torture. Her heart bore enough scar tissue without opening it up to fresh injuries. "If you'll recall, we tried that arrangement for five years and it didn't work."

"I wasn't advocating a reconciliation, just a place for you to sleep. Unless, of course, you have a long lease at that fancy motel of yours."

Hugh had lowered his voice on *fancy* and let loose with a fleeting smirk. With all his faults, gloating hadn't been one of them. Apparently it was now. He was taking fiendish glee in the fact her standard of living had worsened.

No matter how much she'd tried to conceal her difficulties, it didn't take much imagination to deduce from her choice of lodgings that she was low on funds. But it galled her that Hugh had readily done so. "That's temporary," she said defensively.

"Moving back here would be, too. Count on it."

"Charming as your invitation sounds, I must refuse." Leslie pointedly looked at her watch. "It's getting late," she said dismissively. "If I may use the telephone to call a cab, I'll be on my way. You can phone me about the house tomorrow."

"And say what? There's no buyer in sight and the only solution I can propose is that you live here while we try to unload it." The smirk reappeared. And lingered.

"Maybe you'll come up with a better solution by tomorrow. I know *I'll* be giving it a lot of thought." She stood up and started for the telephone.

"Forget the cab," he said. "If you'll hold on ten minutes while I freshen up, I'll drive you to the hotel."

"You don't have to freshen up for me."

"It's not for you. Actually, I'm going out this evening."

"Oh, I should have known—duty calls. What client is it this time? That millionaire playboy who can't brush his teeth without checking with you first, or the lonely widow who's been settling her husband's estate for the past ten years? Did they tag along when you left TGT?"

"Like I said, I'll drive you, but I suggest you mind your manners on the way. I don't intend to listen to a litany of complaints about my law practice anymore. Besides, who said anything about business...maybe I have a date."

Do you? It was a question Leslie knew she couldn't ask. Not that she believed him anyway. Hugh had been too entrenched as the consummate workaholic to pay attention to her, his wife, much less to other women. Now that he had his own firm, he was probably worse than ever. Hugh's advancing the notion of a date was likely a new tactic to aggravate her. He seemed to enjoy punching her buttons tonight.

"Then I'm positive she's anxiously awaiting your arrival," Leslie said. "Go pretty yourself up and I'll browse through a magazine." She grabbed *Sports Illustrated* from a stack on the coffee table and began leafing through the pages. There, that should tell him she didn't give a flip about what he did or whom he saw.

Hugh headed upstairs with Fritz trailing after him. Once he was out of sight, Leslie's body sagged like a deflated beach ball. She was truly wilted from this reunion and cast the unread magazine aside, unable to concentrate because of the emotions overtaking her.

She heard the sound of the shower; it led to other memories, days when she'd lie in bed and wait for him to finish and join her.... *Get hold of yourself*, she scolded. There was nothing to be gained by yearning for what was.

Leslie picked up the magazine and tried to focus again. Fortunately, Fritz's leaping into her lap provided a much-needed distraction. "Hi, fella. Did you come down to entertain me?"

The dog answered with a wag of the tail, then raced off toward the kitchen, halting at the closed door. Leslie, thinking he might be thirsty, pursued, pushed the swinging door open for him and stopped in her tracks. Whoa!

She'd never seen the room cluttered like this. The Hugh she knew wouldn't have tolerated such disarray for thirty seconds. There were stacks of dirty dishes on the countertop keeping company with a Wheaties box, a lidless jar of instant coffee, used tea bags and blackened bananas. Old newspapers lay piled in a corner, jogging shoes under the table, mail and circulars on top.

"You in here?" As he saw her inspection, Hugh's expression became sheepish. "I wasn't expecting visitors," he explained.

"You don't bring your dates home?"

"Not to the kitchen."

"I can see why. This room looks like your worst nightmare."

"Yeah," he admitted, "it is a little messy."

"*Little* messy? What happened to Mr. Clean? Are you really Hugh Campbell?"

"Guilty as charged."

"Well, that's a relief. For an instant, I thought spacemen had kidnapped you and left an alien clone in your place, a sloppy alien clone."

"Okay, okay, you've had your fun," he said. "But feel free to help clean up."

"No way."

He grinned good-naturedly. "Well you can't blame a guy for trying."

If he kept up the grinning, she might help him with the chore—or do anything else he wished. "Are you ready to go?" she asked, trying to remain on an even keel.

"Let me feed the mutt first. I plugged his getaway hole under the fence, so he should be okay for the rest of the evening." Hugh filled plastic bowls with dog food and fresh water.

Leslie studied him as he tended to the dog. He'd changed into a red polo shirt and jeans and she noted with interest his more muscular physique and the tan on his arms. Unlike her, Hugh was not athletic or outdoorsy; his head was generally buried in a law book or bent over the computer keyboard, composing a legal brief. Obviously he'd begun frequenting a gym and grabbing some sun by the backyard pool.

The waft of familiar cologne in her nostrils, Hugh's scrubbed, freshly-shaven face and that smile she'd just glimpsed undermined her last shred of resolve. Believing she could be indifferent to him was nothing but self-delusion. A year—or ten years—apart didn't matter. The truth was in front of her eyes. Now that she'd seen him again, she knew she wouldn't easily get over Hugh Campbell—if she ever could.

Acknowledging her feelings about Hugh was one thing, being isolated in a car with him, quite another. Still, a ride to the motel beat taking a taxi. Soberly acquiescent, Leslie retrieved her purse from the living room and followed Hugh out the rear door into the garage.

She stopped, surprised by the car—a sport-utility van. "Where's the red Miata?"

"I traded it in for this Suburban. What did you think," he asked testily, "that you'd blow into town like a stealth missile and find every detail—down to my wheels—exactly the same as when you left?"

Leslie didn't know what to think. Hugh loved the snazzy Miata, claiming it contributed to the image of an up-and-coming young attorney. Who knew what sort of image Hugh was trying to project with this behemoth.

"No smart answer?" Hugh needled.

"Of course I didn't expect things to be the same," she finally managed.

"Well, good. Dallas didn't go into a time warp just because you disappeared."

Stung by his scolding, she didn't answer. How

quickly Hugh's animosity could resurface. And he was acting as if he had been the one wronged.

After climbing into the van and driving off, neither spoke, the silence of the trip lasting until they neared the motel. "Ah, here we are," Hugh announced sarcastically. "Home sweet home. We must be early—I don't see any ladies of the night out front yet."

"It's not that kind of place," she huffed.

"You could have fooled me."

She hopped out of the car intentionally ignoring his parting shot. "Goodni—" she started to shout, but he got out of the car, too, and began closing in behind her. "This isn't necessary," she complained as Hugh took her arm.

"I think it is." He glanced around, frowning. "Wouldn't you prefer the house to this dump?"

Leslie turned her key in the lock and leaned against the doorjamb. "But that might put a giant kink in your new lifestyle. How would it look for you to be running around on dates with a *wife* waiting at home?"

"Consider it my problem, not yours." His voice lowered to a near whisper and his eyes seemed a softer gray as he studied her face. "Think about it, Les." He propped a hand above her head, and for a moment Leslie hoped...feared he was going to pull her into his arms. If he did, she'd be putty in his hands. But he didn't. Instead, he surprised her by stepping back and waiting for her to get inside. Then he turned and bounded down the steps to his car.

She closed and secured the door, heaving a troubled sigh. The dreaded encounter was over, but the relief she'd anticipated hadn't materialized. She felt more bewildered than relieved.

Nothing that had happened tonight made sense, but

Leslie was too weary for conjecture. Propped in front of a mindless sitcom on TV, she nibbled on a late meal of fruit and a peanut butter sandwich, all purchased from the next-door food mart, then languidly prepared for bed, gratefully crawling between the fresh sheets.

Tired though she was, sleep wouldn't come. Her restive brain kept returning to Hugh. Now that she'd gotten that initial awkward meeting out of the way, what she needed to do was concentrate on restoring her equilibrium. She would do that by fixating on anything but Hugh. The fact that she still loved him was irrelevant. People survived losing at love. She was no clinging vine, no weak-kneed ninny who couldn't live without Hugh Campbell.

Tomorrow she'd begin anew. First contact Byers Textiles about reinstatement in her former job, then seek out an apartment—small, inexpensive and preferably requiring no deposit.

Hugh had suggested not once, but twice, that she share the house. A nonsensical notion to be sure, but one that'd definitely ease her money crunch. Maybe it wasn't so nonsensical. If only the proposition didn't include a mega-dose of Hugh.

"You're back!" Bert Byers barked into the telephone. "I was beginning to think you'd disappeared off the face of the earth. Nice to know you haven't forgotten us." Even though his words were gruffly chiding, Leslie heard pleasure in his voice. Owner of the company she'd worked for, Bert had been her boss, but more than that, her confidant, her buddy. She felt a twinge of guilt that she hadn't kept in touch, the twinge sharper when Bert added, "I worried about you, kiddo."

"I'm sorry. I should have called or written."

"Yes, you should have."

"I thought about you a lot." Maybe it was because he was old enough to be her father that they'd shared such a close bond. Bert, happily married with two grown sons, had undoubtedly savored being a father figure to a daughter, filling the gap left years ago by her own dad's death.

Bert was the person who'd heard Leslie's complaints that Hugh was a replica of her father—burning too much midnight oil and not getting enough enjoyment out of life. Bert was the one who listened while she articulated her fears that Hugh would end up like Victor Baxter, working himself into a coronary.

Yet, sympathetic as Bert was, he hadn't understood—*really* understood—why she was unhappy enough to leave Hugh. "So, what's happening with you?" he asked. Leslie could hear the concern in his voice through the phone line.

"I'm home and I'm job hunting." She took a sip of coffee she gotten from the motel lobby. It was old and burnt and tasted awful. "What's available?"

"Not much. Times are rough. We're still doing some foreign business, but not nearly as much as before."

The news was discouraging and she didn't want to put Bert on the spot, but desperation overrode any hesitancy. "Did you fill my job?"

"Nope, couldn't afford to. Most of our interpreting and translating is being farmed out to consultants."

"What are my chances of getting a piece of that consulting action?" She held her breath.

Leslie could imagine the frustrated shrug of Bert's shoulders. Anyone but Bert would have answered,

"Slim and none." Instead he said, "Why don't you come by tomorrow morning and we'll talk."

After promising to be there at ten, Leslie rang off, wondering what to do next. Apartment hunting was a waste of effort until she nailed down a job. One thing was certain, however, remaining at the Resort Inn wasn't an option, either. Matter of fact, she had few options.

Even here in her hometown, not many people could be imposed upon for help with her particular problem. Calling her mother was out, too. Louise Baxter had remarried and moved to Seattle with her husband, a stern, tight-fisted man, who'd be adamantly opposed to offering Leslie financial assistance or any other type of aid. She was on her own.

And in the cold light of day, Leslie recognized it would be insane to move in with Hugh. Her only recourse was to land a job as fast as possible and put pressure on Hugh to get rid of the house. She dialed his office.

"Serena Blake is a witch," Leslie mumbled to herself as she held the receiver. It had taken five minutes and a threat to keep calling just to get through to him. Leslie longed to burn Hugh's ears with her frank assessment of his irksome secretary. But she didn't want to get sidetracked from her mission. "Are you free for lunch?" she purred.

"You buying?"

Hugh has turned into a major pain. Swallowing an insult, she answered sweetly. "Naturally," she said, praying he'd pick up the bill anyway. "I did the inviting, didn't I?" Today wasn't going to be a repeat of last night, with wall-to-wall sparring. She'd just keep the "catching more flies with honey" adage in mind and try to stay sweet.

"I suppose I can get away," he said, "but it'll have to be late, and brief, too. One-thirty okay? I'll pick you up."

Why had he brought her here, of all places? Memories of the French bistro on Mockingbird Lane had always stirred up a warm nostalgia which Leslie had vaulted away for self-protection. This small corner restaurant with its bustling clientele of students, businesspeople, and matrons—young and old—was where they'd first met while still students at Southern Methodist University. Leslie was pursuing a bachelor's degree with majors in French and Spanish and Hugh was attending law school.

On that special day, he'd been coming in the restaurant with a mutual acquaintance just as she was leaving. Introductions were made and every cliché of love at first sight came to fruition as they gazed into each other's eyes. She and Hugh had spent few days apart after that. Until....

Leslie was staring at her menu but not seeing it. As she struggled to tamp down the wrenching memories, a waitress assisted by interrupting to take their orders. The respite was only fleeting, the memories immediately reemerging as she recalled the many hours spent in this very spot, sitting exactly as they were now, happily mapping out their lives. Even the idea of a belated honeymoon in Paris had begun here, triggered by the French countryside photos on the walls. It had all seemed so perfect then.

"I talked to Bert this morning," she said, determined to cease fixating on the past.

"Oh?"

"Regarding a job. I'm meeting with him tomorrow."

"Then you're planning to stay in Dallas?"

Whether Hugh was pleased or annoyed at the prospect she couldn't tell, so she shrugged noncommittally. It wasn't an easy task to act unruffled what with the butterflies in her stomach, and Leslie felt rescued again when the waitress arrived with a tray of food.

She was reminded of Bogart and Bergman toughing out an emotional reunion in the movie *Casablanca*. If Hugh could stand this, then she could darn well stand it, too. At least there was no Muzak playing "As Time Goes By." "The food is as delicious as ever," she said after a taste of her tomato soup.

He nodded.

"Do you come here often?"

"It's been a long time. Not since..." he chuckled, "since we had that fight over the cheesecake. Remember?" He touched the top of her hand for a moment.

"How could I forget," she said, trying to ignore the touch. "The waiter brought the only remaining piece and you tried to persuade me to order a tart so you'd have it all for yourself."

"Not true. I did offer to split."

"With you getting a Texas-size portion and me getting Rhode Island, then justifying it by saying the larger person got the larger share."

"As usual, you're exaggerating, Les. Besides, you're the one who ranted and raved and swept the whole piece off the table."

"I was not ranting and it was an accident."

He laughed even more. "I'll never forget your expression when the waiter slipped on the fallen cake and dropped a tray of dishes. And you hissing, 'See what you made me do.'"

She joined in the laughter. "I was so embarrassed. I'm surprised they let us back in today."

After a couple of minutes of shared merriment, Hugh took her hand in his, rubbing his thumb across her knuckles. "Can you imagine us fighting over something that silly?"

"No."

"We fought over a lot of things," he said solemnly. "But to be honest, occasionally I miss times like that, the good times."

I even miss the bad times, Leslie admitted silently.

The meal was finished and they were dawdling over dessert—*two* pieces of cheesecake—and coffee. Hugh, despite his declaration about a quick lunch, appeared no more anxious to rush off than she. "It's good to see you eat," he said. "I worr—wondered if you'd been on a crash diet. You're so much thinner, almost waiflike."

Leslie rolled that comment around on her tongue. *Waiflike.* Once upon a time those words would have been heaven to a woman five foot seven who'd always fought to keep the pounds off. But after the illness and subsequent weight loss, Leslie no longer valued thinness—not this kind, anyway—and she doubted that Hugh was paying her a compliment.

"Surprising you lost weight," he continued, "on a diet of French cuisine."

"French, except for the occasional 'Le Big Mac,'" she corrected, taking another bite of the cheesecake, pleased that the rich dessert hadn't made her queasy.

Leslie's doctors had cautioned her about the importance of balanced meals and she'd followed their advice religiously. Recently, however, she'd had little tolerance for food, her apprehension about contacting Hugh stunting her appetite. No need for her to analyze why that was different today. For an hour, both of them had let down their guard and been transported back to those halcyon days when trouble seemed unthinkable.

Hugh finished his last bite of dessert. "Does tomorrow's job interview mean you're thinking of coming home? 'Home' in a manner of speaking," he amended. He scooted his chair away from the table and crossed one leg over the other.

"I suppose I could," she said, returning what she read as a dare in his eyes. "After all, it is half mine."

"True enough," he agreed with a casual wave of the hand. The hand became an imaginary knife. "We can divide it right down the middle. A bedroom for me, a bedroom for you and so on and so on…an even split. But, one exception."

"Oh?"

"I get a larger share of the kitchen. That shouldn't bother you since you retired from cooking anyhow."

As intended, the barb stung. Her hackles rose. *Not that again.* Admittedly, in their last year together, she'd quit trying. Cooking and laundry, her agreed-upon tasks, went undone. For a while, he'd suffered in silence, uttering no comments about his empty sock drawer, and microwaving endless TV dinners without complaint. Near the end, however, he'd begun to speculate aloud if the stove and washer were broken.

"I see you're going to divide the house the same way you did the cheesecake. Well, no matter. You're quite welcome to that eyesore of a kitchen I saw last night. Once it's cleaned up, I may want to renegotiate. For the time being, it's all yours.

"And since you're determined to resurrect the past, I'll remind you that even a short-order cook would have hollered uncle at having to keep food edible for hours on end, never knowing whether dinner would be at seven, eight or midnight.''

"Still on that, are we? Don't you think it's time you quit harping about my hours?"

"You're the one dredging up old gripes."

"And I'm the one who's ending the discussion. What's the point anyway? It's not as if we're a couple anymore."

"So we aren't a couple—actually I've been curious about that. What are we exactly?" She leaned across the table to stare into his eyes. "Has our divorce gone through? How about an update, *Counselor*?"

She took a sip of water, returning to a pose of indifference. Inside, the butterflies were taking flight again. In her goodbye note she'd asked Hugh to have divorce papers drawn up. No big chore since he was with a law firm. And in Texas, filing could be completed and the decree granted in a matter of months.

But she hadn't been served and she reckoned that he couldn't legally terminate their marriage without her consent. Surely she would have had to sign something, or at a minimum be notified.

Hugh moved his chair close in and folded his arms on the table in front of him. "Well, *officially*, we are still a couple. Now that you're here in Dallas, are you going after that marital freedom you wanted so badly?"

For a moment Leslie could have sworn she saw anxiety flash swift as lightning across Hugh's face after he posed the question, but his expression was now bland. "I suppose one of us should eventually," she answered, trying to suppress a pang of sorrow. "Are you in a rush to be available?" She couldn't help herself. She had to know.

"Maybe, maybe not." The surprise appearance of

a devilish grin threw Leslie into an emotional tailspin. "There's a lot of protection in being able to fall back on the matrimonial bit when a woman starts getting ideas," he said.

Hugh made a show of glancing at his watch. "I've got a client due within the hour, so I'd appreciate your making a decision on the house. Now would be nice."

She didn't speak. That "matrimonial bit" comment was still stuck in her craw, and now she was even more steamed at him for foisting a deadline upon her.

"Well?" Hugh prompted.

He wants me to say no. That's why he threw down the gauntlet and picked another fight. He can appear noble, yet force me to turn him down. "I haven't made up my mind. Besides, what's the rush?"

"Can you afford to dally? You're apparently broke, no job yet. Correct?"

Before Leslie could answer, he added, "No rich boyfriend?"

Interesting question. She was mulling over her response when he stood. "Just give me the signal and I'll take you to the motel to get your stuff."

This was happening too fast. She shook her head at the irony of it all. *I can't believe this is me, Leslie Campbell, a.k.a. Leslie the impetuous, alarmed about Hugh's being too hasty.* Yet she wasn't ready. She could bluster all she wanted about returning to live with him, but actually taking the step was quite frightening—and exhilarating, too.

She must have been mistaken thinking he didn't want her to accept. Hugh wouldn't keep repeating his offer if he didn't mean it. His motivation, however, was unclear. Regardless of his denial last night, could Hugh possibly see cohabitation as a step toward reconciliation?

Whatever the stimulus, Leslie had to consider the direction best for her, for both of them. She'd become more cautious in the past year, more alert to the ramifications of her actions. "I'd better look into that job first," she told him. "I'll give you a call after I talk to Bert."

"Les, no matter what Bert says, the practical thing is for you to stay at the house. Can't you see that?" he asked, as though exasperated with the conversation.

Then another possibility dawned on her and Leslie cringed. *He feels sorry for me.* She'd been flattering herself by interpreting his gesture as an olive branch when in truth it was simple pity. He'd made it obvious with the references to her troubles—only she hadn't been paying attention. "Didn't you mention getting back to your office?" she said frostily.

He frowned at his watch. "Oh, man. We should have left for your motel twenty minutes ago. On second thought, why don't you drop me off and take the car. You'll need a way to get to your interview tomorrow."

More charity. "I can't impose on you like that. You need transportation, too."

"Not to worry. Serena will chauffeur me."

Leslie gritted her teeth at the mention of his secretary's name, but made no comment. She *would* need a car. Hugh took her silence as assent, as he hurriedly settled the bill and shepherded her to the car for the drive downtown.

Traffic on Central Expressway was as hectic as ever, with construction and a fender-bender accident creating a massive slowdown. It gave Leslie a chance to study the scenery. Actually there'd been other opportunities, but she'd been too preoccupied to notice.

Now she was taking it in so as to divert her attention from Hugh.

It was June and rather balmy, the oppressive heat of a Texas summer yet to come. The sun-worshiping crepe myrtles were in abundant bloom, their white and fuchsia and lavender blossoms decorating parks and office complexes flanking the roadway.

Dallas hadn't changed significantly in the year she'd been gone, and Hugh—take away a couple of superficial alterations—hadn't, either. Only *she* was different.

The pre-France Leslie had often acted before thinking, and some of those actions had embarrassed Hugh. Childish things, things she regretted. Too, she'd always been a dreamer. So much so that her expectations of marriage had been unrealistic.

Even that stupid desire for an anniversary trip to Paris had been part of a fantasy. Since childhood she'd nursed a wanderlust, wanting to travel the world, live in exotic locations. Her college training and a few trips on a shoestring budget had prepared her for exactly that. Then she'd met Hugh and willingly abandoned her plans.

But eventually a trace of resentment crept in. She had been the one giving up her dreams. Hugh's life had rolled along exactly as projected. Hired by a top Dallas law firm, on the fast track to partnership, while she grew more unhappy by the year. Perhaps if she'd owned up to the resentment earlier they could have dealt with it together—before it became a festering cancer eating away at their marriage.

In the main corridor of Dallas, a few blocks off the expressway, Hugh slowed the car in front of an office building which was both high-rise and high rent. His new practice intrigued her, the fact he'd risked striking out on his own. That wasn't Hugh-like. She couldn't fathom his gambling with such heavy stakes.

Hugh opened the car door and she slid over into the driver's seat. "Do you know how to get to the Resort Inn from here?"

She made an agitated face. "I wasn't out of the country that long." In truth, it'd seemed like eons since she'd left. She wondered if Hugh had experienced the same tortuous passage of time.

"Sorry I asked."

"If you have any idea when you'll be ready to leave, I'll be happy to pick you up," she said, in a conciliatory mode. She appreciated his thoughtful loan of the car. The least she could do was be pleasant about it.

"No need."

"What about tomorrow morning? I—"

"Like I said, I can hitch a ride with Serena. See you…whenever…."

Leslie pulled away from the curb. "Whenever…." His words destroyed any left-over illusions she might have. Regardless of his offer to let her live at the house, Hugh was telling her loud and clear that he was a free agent. She had no hold on him anymore and he no longer considered it necessary to report in to her as his wife. It might not be a courtesy she had any right to expect—but that didn't keep Leslie from feeling as though gray clouds had passed over the sun, obscuring the vibrant day.

CHAPTER THREE

LESLIE spent a restless afternoon and evening and an even more unsettling night. Sleep brought no release. Her dreams were beset with unpleasant images... Leslie begging for Hugh's benevolence, he contemptuous, commenting snidely about her adventures. The dreams descending into the nightmarish—Hugh with another woman, the two engaged in intense lovemaking.

By morning Leslie could hardly wait for the minutes to pass so she could exit this cell of a room for her interview. Hopefully, seeing Bert and visiting her former colleagues would rescue her from the preoccupation with Hugh. Best to shove him from her thoughts right now and concentrate on how good it would be to see those familiar faces.

As though blessed with telepathy and determined to thwart her bid for escape, Hugh called. "Good morning. I wanted to make sure you didn't oversleep."

"Are you that anxious for me to be employed?" Leslie retorted.

"Only because I'd hate to see you on the dole."

"How sweet. But you know what?—selling the house would alleviate that problem really fast. If you're so concerned about my welfare, why don't you devote your energies to that effort?" Darn his hide. Leslie didn't want to keep sparring with Hugh, yet he always seemed to be lying in wait, ready with another one of his well-placed jabs.

"Getting a job will be the best solution for your woes at the moment. And a lot more doable than unloading a house. Shall I call Bert and give you a glowing recommendation?"

"Why do I have the feeling any recommendation from you would be somewhat less than glowing? Besides, you're hardly an expert as far as my skills are concerned."

"I'd say I was *extremely* expert. Unless those… skills…have become impaired during the past twelve months."

Leslie had half a mind to hang up. This conversation was headed downhill faster than an Olympic bobsled. "What are you up to with the needling, Hugh? Trying to get back at me? Well, forget it. I'm immune to your gibes—and to you."

"Are you, Les?" he said in his familiar drawl. "Perhaps we should test the level of your immunity."

"Perhaps we shouldn't." At the sound of his soft laughter, she hung up. *Oooh the nerve of that man.* Before she vented her anger by throwing something, she took the safe route and rushed out the door. She'd have breakfast and read the morning paper somewhere, somewhere Hugh couldn't call and rile her.

Hugh placed the phone back in the cradle and stared at it wonderingly. *Now what did I go and do that for?* Concerned over Leslie's appearance yesterday and the day before—her weight loss and the unusual paleness of her skin—he'd called to make sure she was okay. But he couldn't seem to keep his comments in check. His elation at seeing her again competing with his resentment over being abandoned merged into a churning mass of emotions so that what flowed from his mouth came nowhere near representing how he felt. Heaven help him if she was around when he was in court. He'd blow every case.

However, providence seemed to be leaning his way. At least Leslie hadn't jumped at that rash proposal of his that she move into the house—a proposal he kept reissuing in spite of himself. Too bad providence couldn't take up permanent residence to keep him from speaking when he shouldn't.

Hugh knew cohabitating with her would only make matters worse. Leslie's moving out once had been bad enough. He couldn't endure a second go-round.

"Hi, kiddo!" Bert greeted her the moment she walked in, as if he'd been watching from the window for her arrival. "Welcome home." He gave her a hug, perhaps not a politically-correct greeting for a boss, but appreciated by Leslie nonetheless.

Bert pulled an armchair over to his desk and motioned her to sit down. After spending the next ten minutes describing office changes and updating her on his family, complete with pictures, he got down to business. "Are you back for good?"

"I don't know," she said.

He made a clicking sound with his tongue, the same sort of sound he'd always made when assimilating information.

"A lot depends on you," she blurted out. "On whether I have a job." If he couldn't hire her, Leslie wasn't certain what she was going to do—or where she might go.

He pulled out a drawer to prop his foot on, western boots showing beneath the suit pants. His dark eyes assessed her as he played with his moustache, grayer than last year, Leslie noticed. "Would you consider two days a week for starters? At half your old salary?''

"Half the hourly, or half the monthly rate?''

He laughed. "Half the monthly. Since you'll only be working two-day weeks, technically it's a raise.''

Leslie smiled. Bert Byers and his technicalities. Trying to convince her that two days' work was a raise. Still, it was better than nothing, and she knew Bert was putting himself out. "Thanks," she said. "You're an angel.''

He chuckled. "Your hiatus has done wonders for my standing. You used to call me 'that old devil' more often than not. Now let's talk about your starting date. How's next Tuesday? Thursday could be your second day.''

"That's perfect. It'll give me a chance to find an apartment and—''

"An apartment?" Bert interrupted. "Oh…" he caught himself, "I see.''

Leslie detected a host of pent-up questions in Bert's expression. Especially the obvious one: *What about you and Hugh?* How many women left their husbands and moved away, then showed back up a year later? How many women went begging for a job from the very boss who'd told them they were nuts for walking out? Even though the questions hadn't been posed, Leslie felt compelled to provide some kind of response. "Hugh says hello," she began. "He's heavily involved in his practice, as I'm sure you know.''

Bert nodded and she wished she could discover just how much he *did* know. Hugh was Bert's personal lawyer and handled legal work for the firm. Since the two men were also friends, Bert had to have knowledge about Hugh's life.

"So you'll be living alone?''

"Hugh made overtures about my staying at the house, but that would just revive our problems." She gave Bert a condensed version of recent happenings. "So you see, a year's separation hasn't changed anything."

"A year of *avoiding* your problems hasn't changed anything, you mean," Bert said. "Don't you think the time has come to face them? You two still love each other."

"You're wrong about that, Bert. From what I've seen, Hugh's been doing famously without me." *My life's the one in shambles.*

"If everything's so hunky-dory for him, then why did he suggest you move back in?"

"Because he feels sorry for me, that's why. 'Poor Leslie. She frittered away all her money and needs good old Hugh to lend a helping hand.' He as good as told me he didn't plan on a reconciliation."

"I find that hard to believe."

"Well, he did."

"Still…just because he said it, doesn't prove he meant it. Why don't you take him up on his offer to stay at the house? See what develops. I dare you." He tugged at his mustache again. "Or are you too much of a coward?"

Recognizing the taunt for what it was, Leslie shook her finger at Bert. "You know I'm usually a pushover for a challenge, but not this time. You can't sucker me into this, Bert Byers."

Bert harrumphed, his bushy brows rising. "If you're not up for dares, then how about lunch?" He gave her a quick once-over. "We have to fatten you up some. You've got about as much meat on you as a coatrack. What do you say? The restaurant down the street grills a great chicken sandwich. Terrific fries, too.''

Knowing she would likely be grilled along with the chicken, Leslie postponed the lunch until Tuesday. As much as she adored Bert, she'd endured enough discussion about her relationship with Hugh for one day and had no intention of giving chapter and verse about her health, which was where Bert was headed next. Leslie bade him goodbye, spent a few minutes chatting with the staff, then left for the motel, stopping off for a chef salad along the way.

As she drove down Preston Road and turned onto LBJ Freeway, Bert's words kept playing in her mind. Maybe she should put pride aside and consent to Hugh's proposition. Hugh was right in one area—she was broke.

The part-time salary she'd earn with Bert would scarcely cover transportation, food and incidentals. Leslie had no idea how she'd manage rent, too, and any more medical expenses would plunge her into bankruptcy. Staying with Hugh, she'd be able to squirrel away a bit of her earnings and line up a second job—maybe teaching a language course—to supplement her income. Sufficient reason to put up with the man she'd been married to for five years, Leslie told herself, refusing to acknowledge those more tantalizing reasons for moving back in.

By the time she reached the motel, she'd convinced herself. Reluctantly, she dialed Hugh. Best to ensure that his offer had no strings attached and then accept. If she could get through his pit bull of a secretary, that is. Ready to do battle with Serena, Leslie was surprised when Hugh himself answered. ''Hugh Campbell.''

"Uh, hello," she said, confusion evident in her voice, "it's you."

"So you decided you're not so immune to me after all?" Hugh drawled.

"How you do flatter yourself," Leslie retorted. "Actually, I've been thinking about the house."

"Oh, not more real estate talk. You're becoming a real bore on that topic."

"Hear me out before you start attacking. I want to take you up on your suggestion."

"And what suggestion is that?"

Hugh was being deliberately dense. "Sharing the house of course."

"Who says the offer's still open?"

"Quit trifling with me, Hugh. Or are you honestly trying to tell me you've changed your mind?"

"Hmm, I'm not sure. I'll think it over and let you know."

"How about letting me know right now?"

"Can't. A client's waiting. I'll give you a call when I get home tonight. 'Bye."

"Wait a minute there." Leslie felt the blood rushing to her head. Hugh Campbell got more maddening by the hour. "If you think you can dangle that invitation before me, then renege once I've agreed, you've got another think coming. There's no way you can keep me out of *my* house. I've even got a key now—the one on your key chain."

"Like I said, we'll talk about it later."

Leslie was certain she could detect amusement in his voice. Hugh seemed to get his kicks these days from giving her a rough time. Well, she'd show him.

"We have talked. Consider it a done deal." She hung up before Hugh could get in another word.

Swiftly packing her belongings, she glanced around

to make sure she hadn't overlooked anything, tossed her suitcase into the car, then stopped by the motel office to check out.

Thirty minutes later, she was easing into her old driveway, the familiar act creating a wrenching ambivalence. One part of her warmed to the naturalness of the motion, yet another part protested that she didn't belong here—not any longer.

Leslie unlocked the side door and entered, pulling the wheeled-suitcase like a dog on a leash. "Speaking of dog...Fritz, where are you?" Hearing the summons, the furry dynamo bounded through his doggie door, ecstatically circling and leaping, his tail wagging wildly. "Well, someone loves me," she said, bending down to stroke the adoring pet. "Why don't you help me unpack?"

His answer was to sit up and beg. "Oh, you want to be paid for your love, do you?" She glanced around the kitchen, wondering where his treats might be. The shambles from the day before was now cleared, the countertops wiped clean, and not so much as a coffee cup marred the orderly scene. A shining sea of Formica, just as Hugh preferred. Leslie rummaged in the cabinets and found the box of dog biscuits, giving one to Fritz before grabbing the strap of her suitcase once more.

Earlier, Hugh had said they would divide the house, but as to where she would sleep, the decision was made for her. Of the four bedrooms upstairs, only two had been furnished, one as the master bedroom and one for guests.

She opened the door to the guest bedroom. It was exactly the same, a pine-framed bed with a plum-colored bedspread, a nightstand and lamp and a rocking chair. Not lavishly decorated, but neat and inviting for a guest, and for her now, too. She parked the suitcase in a corner and lay down on the bed. It was only four, but she was spent from the day's exertion.

Again she slept fitfully, dreaming one dream after another. She was back in college, then here, then in Paris sick in bed. Hugh was in Paris, too, coming to stand by her and saying, "What have we here?"

Leslie sighed pitifully and he sat on the bed, solicitously taking her hand. She reached out to touch his face, caressing it, and he tenderly bent down to brush his lips against hers.

His lips felt so good, so soft, so wonderfully familiar. She wrapped her arms around him, savoring the physical reunion. He still had the faint aroma of aftershave; she could smell it on his neck.

Smell it! Leslie's eyes popped open to discover Hugh's only inches away. "What are you doing in here?"

"I might ask you the same question, Sleeping Beauty."

She sat up. His tone was soft, gentle, but it didn't prevent her from recalling their last conversation. "I think it's pretty obvious that I've moved back in. Did you honestly think I'd still be sitting by the phone at the Resort Inn waiting for your permission?"

"Of course not." All gentleness vanished from Hugh's voice. "We both know you do what you want, when you want. Actually, though, I was talking about your being in bed."

"I lay down for a little nap, that's all. But I wouldn't have if I'd known you were going to sneak in and try to take advantage of me while I was asleep."

"Now hold it." The pale light seeping in from the hall revealed a fiery glint in Hugh's eyes. "There was no sneaking and no advantage taking. I merely came in here to see if you were okay. It's after eight and you haven't stirred all evening.''

"Oh," she said meekly. "I didn't realize…but that still doesn't account for your kissing me like… like…."

"Like I was accepting an invitation?"

Leslie was indignant. "There was no invitation. I was asleep, remember?"

"And yet so cooperative."

"I was still groggy." Thank goodness she'd finally awakened and put a stop to it. The meaningful look Hugh gave her said he knew exactly how difficult that stopping had been. Hugh wasn't the type of man to take advantage; he might have initiated that kiss, but once his lips had touched hers, Leslie had become an equal partner. Their lovemaking had never been one-sided. Leslie wished she could deny the ache in the pit of her stomach that revealed a stronger-than-ever longing for Hugh. But she couldn't.

"Are you getting up?"

Leslie shook her head. She didn't trust what might happen if she didn't maintain some protective distance right now. "I'm really tired."

Hugh didn't argue. "Then I'll see you in the morning."

Not if I can avoid it, Leslie thought. She lay awake for hours trying to erase the sensation of Hugh from her mind and it was past midnight when she managed to drop off again.

Leslie awakened late the next morning, the bedside clock telling her it was nearing nine. She felt guilty for spending so many hours in bed, but was relieved when she realized that Hugh would have left for the office and she'd avoided dealing with him again. Tonight would be soon enough.

She lingered in the guest bath under a spray of hot, soothing water. Her relief was short-lived, however, for when she emerged from her shower and opened the door to the hall, there was Hugh posing like a well-trained butler, holding a cup of coffee for her. He was already dressed, and uncomfortable was an inadequate word to describe how she, in a state of semi-nudity, felt with him so close.

Hugh stared, studying her as though the thick towel, wrapped sarong-style around her, was transparent. He shook his head disapprovingly. "You're too thin. I liked you with a little more roundness, not so many angles, softer...more touchable."

"Since you're not going to be doing any touching, it hardly matters how you liked me, does it?"

Hugh didn't respond, although his silence said a lot. Leslie felt as if he were touching her right then and, remembering her all-too-eager response to him last night, she began to blush, her face threatening to match her pink towel.

He handed her the coffee, cleared his throat and said, "Your decision to stay here surprised me."

She gripped the towel tighter and took a sip of the coffee. "As I've said before, the house is half mine. There's plenty of extra room, and I've decided to make use of it."

"Until you get the urge to run off again."

She shot him a hundred-volt glare. "This arrangement is going to be intolerable for both of us unless you contain that tongue of yours."

"I can't make any promises on that," Hugh said unapologetically. He crossed his arms in front of him. "It's been pretty quiet around here without your erratic behavior. Don't blame me if it brings out my bad side.''

''I'm *not* erratic,'' Leslie answered, having difficulty putting as much spirit into the denial as she would have liked. Her actions had been rather...uh, changeable in the past. Not just her proclivity for throwing handy household items, but dozens of other not-so-adult behaviors...months of frenetic job hopping before settling in at Byers, deliberately washing red towels with Hugh's white undershorts tinting them a pale pink, stunts to get Hugh's attention like driving off to Padre Island for the weekend without letting him know. However, if he thought the past was an indicator of future behavior patterns, he was mistaken.

All of that was behind her now. She was more mature, more consistent than a year ago, a late-blooming grown-up. No point in telling him that though and listening to him scoff. He'd find out for himself eventually, and in the interim she could enjoy keeping him guessing. Her towel started slipping and Leslie had to clutch it with one hand while trying to keep the coffee she held in the other from spilling.

Hugh grinned, his amusement at her machinations almost making Leslie forget how mature she was supposed to be now. He opened the bedroom door for her. ''Get dressed and eat some breakfast. You can come to the office with me, then take the car.''

''That's not necessary. I don't want to inconvenience you again.'' She slipped past him into the room, fervently wishing the door had a lock, uneasy that Hugh could walk in whenever he chose. The idea made her dress in record time. He was still waiting when she returned to the hallway.

''Don't be stubborn, Les,'' he continued.

Look who's talking about stubborn. Apparently it

was an attribute he had honed in her absence. Hugh cooling his heels outside her door to finish an argument didn't fit his usual style. He normally leaned more toward indifference or preoccupation when dealing with her, rather than being so willfully tenacious.

"Drive in with me." His tone brooked no dissension. "Serena will bring me home so you don't have to worry about me."

Her again. "I wouldn't worry," Leslie snapped, irritated by his bossiness and even more by another reference to Serena.

"Of course you wouldn't. Foolish assumption on my part. Now hurry up before you make me later than I already am."

"So sorry to interfere with your precious—" Hugh's glare stopped Leslie in midsentence. Why, oh why, had she sold her Toyota a year ago instead of just leaving it in the garage? *To show Hugh you weren't returning. Cutting off your nose just like you're doing now.* Quit arguing and use the dratted car, she told herself. Use it to find transportation of your own and eliminate this continual hassle. She smiled at Hugh. "Yes, thank you. I'd appreciate having the car."

"Good, then it's settled." Hugh grinned, making it plain that he was quite aware her politeness and control were forced.

"Can you give me about five minutes to do my makeup?" she asked.

"I'll give you thirty. Breakfast, remember."

"The coffee's fine. I'll grab a bite later." Even though she'd slept through supper, she was too nervous to think about food right now.

"We're not leaving this house until you eat." He looked her up and down. "That jeans and skimpy blouse outfit conceals none of your boniness. You've been skipping too many meals."

Rather than rebut his statement, Leslie compliantly went along. "Yes, sir. Then I'd better see to that breakfast." She turned toward the stairs and hurried into the kitchen, intent on fleeing from Hugh's observations. But he followed after her.

She frowned at the box of sugar-coated corn puffs on the counter. "Is this kid cereal all you have?"

"The grocery was out of the hard-core adult stuff. Sorry about that, your highness. But feel free to buy your own."

"I will and I'll try not to sponge off you any more than I have to."

He came over and took her by the shoulders. "Look, Les, that's not what I meant."

"A man courtroom-trained to think on his feet having trouble expressing himself? I think not." She shrugged out of his grasp, fearful of turning to mush if he held her too long. "Now why don't you read the paper or something and leave me to my corn puffs?"

"Sure, I'll be glad to." He raised his arms up in the air as if to signify "See, no hands."

She took a carton of milk from the refrigerator while Hugh slipped the morning newspaper from its plastic bag and sat down at the table, scanning the front page. When she reached for the coffee carafe, Hugh lifted his cup signaling for a refill.

It was a simple act, one carried out hundreds of times during their marriage, so there was no rhyme or reason to her feeling the way she did, as fidgety and excited as a teenager who'd been offered a crumb of attention from her school's football hero. Subjecting herself to all this togetherness had been a gigantic miscalculation, but she didn't have any choice except to stay. She would have to endure it, for a few weeks anyway.

"As soon as I do my makeup and brush my teeth I'll be ready," she told him, finishing the last spoonful of cereal. Hugh began straightening the paper to take along.

Fifteen minutes later they were driving downtown, Hugh at the wheel, Leslie determined to keep her mind on the future rather than the past.

"You still haven't told me much about your practice," she ventured, seeking an innocuous topic.

"What is it you want to know? Trying to discover if I'll soon be solvent enough to buy you out instead of selling the house?"

"Let's not fight," she said, a plea in her voice. "Do you have partners, associates?"

"I'm leasing space with one other lawyer, but our practices are separate for now. Serena and a paralegal are my only employees."

Leslie fumed at the way Hugh constantly injected the woman's name into the conversation. He seemed to take every opportunity to mention her, making Leslie wonder whether there was a subtle message there, a message that Serena wasn't just an employee to him. It didn't take an Einstein to conclude that the irritating Ms. Blake desired a more significant role. Maybe she'd already snared Hugh. *Not that I give a hoot.*

When Hugh pulled to the curb and cut the engine, Leslie decided to stop permitting such disgruntled thoughts from preying on her mind. So she and Hugh were to be roommates for a while. It could be quite innocent. She'd simply hark back to her college days and remember how one treated a roomie. As he got out of the car, she called out insincerely, "Have a nice day."

Before Leslie headed for home, she sought out an automobile dealership. The selection of a used Geo and credit arrangements were completed in record time, desperation to have her own vehicle preventing her from scrutinizing every car on the lot. The car would be ready for pick-up the next morning.

That task accomplished, her next stop was the supermarket. She might be living with Hugh, but she wasn't going to freeload any more than necessary.

She picked up a box of vitamin-enriched cereal, juices, some fresh fruit and vegetables, milk and cheese, a bag of brown rice and a salmon steak. If Hugh came home early, they could cook the vegetables and salmon steak on the patio grill. Maybe even swim before supper.

The thought threw Leslie back to the past again. Hugh had been so proud of the pool, looking forward to his evening swims and insisting she join him occasionally. *Maybe the pool isn't such a good idea*, she decided, recalling how those particular swims had ended.

The sun had long since disappeared over the horizon and the moon hung like a soft silver balloon in the darkened sky, but Hugh hadn't come home. She knew he wasn't at the office because Serena had telephoned for him, asking that he call her "the minute he arrives." She obviously hadn't thought Leslie dependable enough to deliver the request because she phoned twice more that evening. Hugh definitely wasn't with Serena. Where was he then?

The planned meal had gone uncooked and Leslie had been too upset from all her speculating to eat.

Now it was after eleven and her stomach was rumbling. She slipped out of bed and pulled on a robe, realizing she'd never get to sleep if she didn't feed the growling tiger within her.

She'd just sliced off a piece of cheese when she heard a car door slam. Dashing to a living-room window, she peered outside, only to see a late-model Corvette with a woman at the wheel, pulling away from the curb. Hugh came sauntering up the sidewalk, his jacket thrown over one shoulder, his white shirt-sleeves rolled up to the elbow. There was no evidence of the briefcase he'd carried that morning and Leslie could swear he was whistling. She raced back to the kitchen to avoid being caught in the act of spying.

"I see your habits haven't changed," she said, layering a cracker with cheese as he joined her in the kitchen. "You're still arriving home in the middle of the night."

Hugh arranged his jacket across a chair back. "But not because of the office." He bent down to scratch Fritz behind the ears. "My *working* late was your gripe. Remember?"

"All too well." She didn't understand why she felt so hell-bent on quarreling with him. Maybe it was because he *hadn't* been at the office tonight. All those years she'd fought unsuccessfully to slow him down so that they could spend more time together. And now he had no compunction whatsoever about partying the night away with another woman. A woman who could afford a new Corvette at that. "If you'd devote as much time to business as you did in the past, perhaps you'd be able to pay me my share of the house."

"You're never satisfied, are you? 'You work too much. You don't work enough'," he mimicked. Hugh stepped closer and hovered over her. "If you're going to live here, you might as well quit nagging. It's going to be quite a while before I have the kind of money needed to buy your slice of the equity. If you want to sell the damn house, then you have a stab at it. But, in the meantime, don't tell me when I can come and go. You lost that privilege when you walked out on me.'' He pulled a can of Sprite from the refrigerator and stalked off.

Leslie slumped into a kitchen chair, dismayed at his outburst. Well at least he wasn't tuning her out. His old method for dealing with marital disagreements was a caustic word or two, then a reminder that he had enough confrontation at work and didn't need it at home. If pushed too far, he usually stormed off to the office or retreated to bed, his back to her when she later joined him.

She mulled over what Hugh had just said. *Had* she nagged? After some quiet deliberation, Leslie begrudgingly admitted to herself that sometimes she had.

During the year in France, she'd often thought of how their relationship had begun to fray at the edges, especially that last year together. She had faulted Hugh for allowing his career to come between them and ruin their happiness. But later she reluctantly recognized how she, too, was at fault. Nothing like months of bed rest and solitude to make a person re-examine her own behavior.

She'd blamed Hugh for so much and refused to see the situation from his point of view. Whether or not she'd had legitimate complaints against her husband was irrelevant. Her approach to their difficulties— shrewish was probably an apt description—had been counterproductive, accomplishing nothing.

As Leslie climbed the stairs to the guest room, she

noticed Hugh's closed door. He had come home looking so self-satisfied after his date tonight. She wondered whether the woman still held his attention. Leslie had egotistically reasoned that her mere presence would banish other females from the scene. Apparently she was quite mistaken.

What's the matter with you? Do you think Hugh's world stops just because you reenter it? Besides, what difference does it make? You tell yourself you don't want him. Don't you want anyone else to have him, either? Is that the kind of woman you've become?

Leslie had no answers. Yet she couldn't keep from pondering about the woman…women in Hugh's life. How many were there anyway? Serena. Tonight's mystery lady. Anyone else? "He certainly lost no time replacing me," Leslie said to Fritz, who'd accompanied her to bed, and was now lying by her side, his shaggy head resting on her arm. The dog edged closer and nuzzled a cold wet nose against her cheek.

Leslie wondered why the animal hadn't trotted off to join Hugh, why he'd remained with her. Maybe in his young puppy days, his owner had been a female. Where had Fritz come from? A gift from one of Hugh's women? No, she quickly decided. A girlfriend would have given a swanker pooch, one with a pedigree. Fritz had animal shelter written all over him. But that was of no concern to Leslie; she'd fallen in love with the ugly mutt. His roots didn't matter.

She did wish he could talk though. So many of her unanswered questions would then be laid to rest. Fritz was a good listener, but limited on the conversation side. So even though she found the dog a most agreeable companion, she'd simply have to wait around until his lord and master chose to tell her about his lady friends—if ever.

*   *   *

The next morning, Leslie asked Hugh to drive her to the dealership so she could pick up her Geo, then she returned home to spend the rest of the day attending to practical matters, namely her office wardrobe.

The bedroom next to hers, empty except for an ironing board and a treadmill, had been envisioned as a nursery. The fourth one was filled with cardboard boxes containing the personal possessions she'd packed before she left. Leslie remembered the tears she had shed as she crammed all the belongings she'd considered ''hers'' into those boxes. It was a marvel they weren't mildewed from all the crying.

She opened one of the unlabeled boxes and started rummaging. Finally locating the clothes, she dragged the boxes to her room and began laying the clothing on the bed so she could get an idea of what she had.

There were three nice summer suits and matching blouses. She tried on her favorite suit, a natural linen, and stared into the mirror. The sight was depressing. The wrinkled jacket didn't look much better on her than it did on the hanger and the skirt was at least two sizes too big. She hadn't realized until this moment how much difference a twenty-five pound weight loss made. She now had the frame of a Paris runway model and the wardrobe to fit a woman athlete. Not a happy combination. She would have to improvise with pins and belts until she either put on some weight or had the income to buy smaller size additions to her collection.

By seven, she was exhausted, aching from her rather undemanding labors of unpacking, washing and ironing. It was at times like these she realized that her healing process wasn't complete. Once she'd had ample energy to hold a nine to five job, then do laundry, cook, and putter in the yard afterward. Once, too, she reminded herself, Hugh had been around to do his part. Today he was gone again and she couldn't help but wonder if he was off on another frolic.

She'd left the house only briefly, dropping clothes by the cleaner's and picking up a box of detergent at the supermarket. During her absence, Hugh had come home and changed. Through his opened bedroom door she saw a tie dangling from the knob of a dresser drawer, his shirt and suit coat thrown across the bed, and the trousers draped over the arm of a chair. His dress shoes lay in the middle of the room, each stuffed with a sock. Whoever he was with right now, Hugh'd been in a mad hurry to join them.

It was dark when he came in, dirtier than Leslie ever remembered him, mud splattered on the front of his T-shirt and cutoffs. A big smile crossed his face as he raised a string of fish for her perusal. "Have you ever seen prettier catfish?"

"Beauty is in the eye of the beholder, obviously."

"You'll change your mind after you taste these beauties mesquite-grilled." He dropped the fish into the kitchen sink and reached for a knife to clean them.

"Took the afternoon off?" she inquired benignly, mindful not to overstep herself this time.

"It's Friday. I fish on Friday."

Since when? she wondered, unable to recall Hugh as a regular participant in any bona fide recreation. Jogging didn't count since the intense way he went at it on his treadmill made the activity more like work than exercise. "Did you fish alone?"

Hugh turned and grinned. "Sounds like you're the one fishing now." He pulled off several paper towels and spread out the catfish fillets. "No, I wasn't alone. Abby was with me."

CHAPTER FOUR

"'ABBY'? The woman who brought you home last night?" Leslie, abandoning her pose of indifference, steered the conversation precisely where Hugh expected her to, and precisely where she shouldn't.

"Aha! You *were* spying on me when I came home." He wagged a finger at her. "Naughty girl."

"Don't be silly," she said, swatting at his hand. "I thought I heard a noise and just happened to see a car driving off as I was glancing out the window."

"Right," he answered patronizingly. "Well, since you're so curious, that was Grace. Abby likes the outdoors and Grace?—well, I know for a fact that Grace hates fishing." He chuckled—an annoying little chuckle in Leslie's opinion—and continued, "Nope, I can't see Grace in fishing gear. She's definitely the diamonds and silk type of woman."

"Gifts from you, I suppose?" *I've done it again. Won't someone gag me before I say anything else?*

"No, I haven't bought her a single gift..." He paused. "Not in my present state. Financial state that is, not matrimonial." Hugh pulled off several paper towels and spread them on the cabinet, ready to drain the fish.

"You're being *very* transparent," Leslie chided. "Really, Hugh," she said, "I think you're trying to make me jealous."

"Oh, is that what I'm doing? Well, am I succeeding?" He turned to face her, his feet anchored on the tile floor, long bare legs stretched out in front of him.

Leslie laughed dismissively, hoping to convince him she didn't care one whit. *Faker.* All too easily Leslie could visualize Hugh with Grace, she in silk…the filmy kind, the kind worn in bedrooms. Was that what it took to get his attention these days? Swathing oneself in silk? Then maybe she ought to buy some. Immediately, Leslie quashed the notion. The last thing she needed was to seduce her husband back into her arms.

This arrangement was temporary—she had to keep remembering that. The problems that had driven them apart still existed. She might be harboring feelings for Hugh, but for her own sake, she had to suppress them. She loved him, *he'd* once loved her—of that Leslie was confident—but it didn't change anything. Love was not a cure-all. If they hadn't made a success of their marriage when love abounded unconditionally, what chance did it have now when they were estranged from one another?

Better to keep their relationship as uncomplicated as possible. Rekindling old fires in the midst of a divorce would definitely be a major complication.

"Shall we grill these?" Oblivious to her thoughts, Hugh had returned to his chores. He held up a fish filet for her perusal. "Or have you already eaten?"

"No, not yet. I'll steam some asparagus while—"

"While I get cleaned up?" he finished for her. "How about potatoes and hot rolls, too? I'm starved."

He lit the gas grill before heading upstairs, leaving a confused Leslie behind. Hugh had been matter-of-fact discussing the other women in his life with her, then equally matter-of-fact resuming old patterns with Leslie.

* * *

The dishes had been cleared away and Leslie and Hugh were sitting at poolside with tumblers of iced tea, a chorus of noisy cicadas serving up background music. Although it was almost nine, the air was humid, the first warning of the hot, sticky months to come.

"Did you miss Dallas summers while you were away?" Hugh's question was seemingly innocuous, but Leslie sensed that their easy rapport was about to undergo a subtle change. She'd left in June, on a day much like this one, with the temperature hovering near the ninety-degree mark.

"The summers were the one thing I didn't miss."

"The one thing? Careful, Leslie. That all-encompassing statement could mean that you missed even me. Of course, we know that isn't true."

"Good thing, too," she retorted. "Since you replaced me so readily. If I take all your hints seriously, then I see you with would-be wives lined up into the next century."

"What was I supposed to do—sit around sucking my thumb and bemoaning your departure?"

"You *could have* visited me. Or dropped a note letting me know you were okay. At least I did send you some cards."

"Oh, and romantic little missives they were. 'Dear Hugh. How are you? I am fine. Here is my current address. Leslie.' No love, not even a clichéd 'wish you were here.' No wonder I didn't rush over."

"Wishing you there would have been self-defeating when you clearly had no interest in joining me. And as far as unromantic is concerned, I'm surprised you noticed, since you'd demonstrated such a strong preference for business over romance."

Instead of a frosty comeback or a frown, Hugh

looked over at her and grinned, pleased he'd stoked her temper so easily. When she'd called Monday, he hadn't known what to expect. *I don't know a hell of a lot more now, but I do know you're not indifferent to me. Ah, Les. I've seen those furtive glances when you think I'm not looking. Those spurts of jealousy too...*

"Speaking of business, have you figured out how to sell the house?" she asked.

"I haven't had time," he said. "Besides, now that you're back, why is it solely my responsibility? As you've pointed out, half of the place is yours. If you're so anxious to get rid of it, then why don't you take my advice and handle the sale yourself. You're the one who's so danged money hungry." He paused thoughtfully. "Strange, since you never appreciated the value of money before."

Leslie didn't respond. In the heavy silence, Hugh drained his tea, then began bouncing the glass on his knee, jiggling the ice cubes and wishing he could retract some of his last comments. Maybe he'd been too harsh. More gently he said, "Was money your only reason for returning, Les?"

She nibbled at her lip, obviously pondering her response. Why can't she just say "no"? Hugh wondered. *Why can't she say she's returned because she still wants me and hopes to salvage our marriage?* If Leslie would admit as much, then he could start forgiving, putting aside some of his anger.

If she'd confess that she regretted going and that she wanted him, then they could begin addressing the problems she ran away from. Possibly avoid a divorce. Jeez, he'd seen enough messy ones in his career to know it wasn't what he wanted for himself. But as things stood, he had to protect himself. He couldn't get his hopes up, then go through the pain and dejection of losing her again.

"What other reason could there be for coming back?" she finally responded. "It sure wasn't to subject myself to your criticism."

He stopped himself from a cruel retort. Leslie was right about the need for him to hold his tongue. Especially since she was as combative as he. The way things were headed they couldn't be in each other's presence without lobbing insults like grenades. This time he'd end the harmful exchange before it went any further. Hugh stood and picked up their glasses. "I think I'll put these in the dishwasher and hit the sack. Fishing's great, but it wears me out."

"You go on to bed," Leslie said. "I'll load the dishes."

"Don't bother, I'm used to doing it." The subtle admonishment escaped before Hugh could stop it. *So much for good intentions. I can't even trust myself.* Right now he had to be away from her, to get his feelings under control before he said something so provocative that this minor skirmish became a full-fledged war, or worse, before he grabbed her and kissed her senseless, making love to her the way he'd wanted to since she'd first appeared at the front door.

"Then I'll say goodnight," she said, the hurt expression in her eyes making him feel like a gold-plated heel.

She was at the foot of the curving staircase when Hugh called her name. He hadn't meant to, but seeing her there, his mind flashed back to the old days, when she started to bed earlier than he and he'd remind her to stay awake for him.

"Yes?" Leslie's voice was husky as she turned around, her liquid brown eyes expectant.

He stepped toward her and for endless moments they stood staring at one another, longing written on both their faces. Hugh forced himself to sever the contact. "Nothing," he said, absently shaking his head. "Goodnight."

It was Saturday morning, but Hugh, dressed in crisp chinos and a sport shirt, was outside when Leslie, still in her pajamas and robe, came downstairs. Opening the French doors, she stepped onto the patio and watched him cutting withered blooms off a climbing rosebush.

She noticed a multitude of new plants—petunias, begonias and hibiscus blooming riotously, even her small vegetable garden along the back fence sprouting new growth.

Apparently Hugh, who—other than mowing—had left the yard work to her, had kept up her gardens. She was surprised and a little touched, too. Gardening was both her hobby and her escape. And here stood the backyard a year later, as beautiful as ever. Someone had given it hours of tender loving care. No, it couldn't be Hugh. He must have taken on a gardener.

"What's going on?" she asked.

"Just tending to the chores, ma'am." He joined her near the French doors. "Before I head off to my day job."

"Are you going to spend the entire weekend at the office to make up for playing hooky yesterday?" she asked grumpily, flopping down at the patio table. Her sleepless night was all Hugh's fault and it hardly seemed fair that he looked so dapper and alert.

"What did you have in mind? Are you hinting that you'd rather have me around?" He curled his hands around the top of a neighboring chair and leaned toward her.

"Not the way you're insinuating," she huffed. "I just wondered if you'd really changed your spots and started enjoying life. Or if yesterday was simply a fluke."

"I'm not sure how to answer that. Let's just say I work hard and play hard these days."

"I suppose that's an improvement. Maybe you won't end up like my father after—"

The amused look vanished and a somber one took its place. "What do you mean 'end up like' your father? He's dead."

"That's right, dead. Dead at forty because he worked himself into an early grave. The same place you were headed."

One of Hugh's eyebrows raised. "Is that the reason you left?"

"Maybe. It's not much fun watching someone working himself to death."

"I suppose you'd have preferred me not to work at all. Like *my* father."

She rolled her eyes. "You're not going to drag your worthless dad into this conversation."

"Why not? You brought up your dad."

"Yes, to make a point."

"Well I have one, too. You can lose a parent to things other than death. My mother can tell you plenty about loss, and about how dear old dad ran out on her."

"Okay, you win. Sloth bad. Work good. Forget I said anything. Just go on to your precious office and do what you do best."

"Thanks for your permission," he said snidely,

storming inside and slamming the door behind him, the tiny French windowpanes shaking in their frames.

Leslie instantly regretted her lapse. She shouldn't have fallen into the trap of attempting to explain herself to Hugh. She'd tried to often enough over the years and yet they always wound up at the same impasse. Hugh never listened to her about his working habits; he'd simply thrown in his devil-may-care father as a counter example. If she hadn't still felt so vulnerable from last night, Leslie wouldn't have bothered with a defense. But the way Hugh had looked at her from the bottom of the stairs had made her hope that perhaps....

More wishful thinking. After Hugh drove off, she went in for a cup of coffee, then stretched out on a patio lounger to drink it. Fritz, ever companionable, stretched out on the ground beside her.

When she'd emptied her coffee cup, she leaned back and clasped her hands behind her head, thinking about Hugh. Leslie knew she should have been grateful he'd left her alone last night. If he'd come one step closer, uttered one conciliatory word, who knew what might have happened? But that didn't alter the disappointment which still stabbed at her heart, or change the hurt from this morning's conversation.

In an effort to divert her thoughts, she glanced around the yard. It did feel good to see that it hadn't gone to seed. A restful scene like this could almost make her forget her frustrations. The flawless lawn, the rectangular pool clear and inviting. She could sit here all day.

Fritz apparently agreed. He was close beside her, sound asleep. The twitching of his muzzle in soft doggy snores brought a smile to Leslie's face as she reluctantly eased herself up. She hated to awaken him, but she needed breakfast.

A bowl of cereal, a glass of juice and she was ready for some physical activity. But there was nowhere she had to go, nothing she had to do, no leisure activity that appealed to her today. A second cup of coffee in hand, she wandered through the house, closely and carefully scrutinizing it from a buyer's point of view.

She paused in the dining room. Aside from the purchase of bed, couch, and appliances, this had been the first room actually decorated. She and Hugh had planned it as a social center, contemplating long conversations with friends and loved ones over home-cooked meals. But that was not to be. Except for a handful of holidays, they'd presided over few gatherings. Now that she thought about it, the room typified one of the flaws in their marriage—good intentions that never materialized.

She ran her fingers over the tabletop. Dusty. And the brass candelabra they'd found at an estate sale wore a heavy coat of tarnish.

Hugh should have invested in a maid as well as a gardener. No doubt about it, the place fairly begged for a good spring cleaning, the neglect quite obvious. Dust balls congregated in the corners and cobwebs clung to all the light fixtures. Leslie permitted herself a moment of pleasure that Hugh, who took to heart the cleanliness-godliness adage, hadn't gotten along without her quite as well as she'd thought.

Unless a home reached the pigsty stage, lack of domestic attention shouldn't doom a turnover. But the cobwebs surely weren't a selling point, either. This place needed a military spit shine to enhance its buyer appeal. Leslie went upstairs to change into shorts and a T-shirt before running out to purchase some serious cleaning supplies.

Veering into the driveway on the return trip, she noticed a woman spraying marigolds in the yard next door. Short gray hair, a stylish jumpsuit, and maturely attractive, she was appraising Leslie with an unrelenting stare. The Voights must have moved during her absence, Leslie guessed, watching the unfamiliar neighbor aim the nozzle of her garden hose at the orange and yellow blooms. She gave a smile to the stranger and received one in reply, although the surveillance continued.

Shopping bag hoisted on her left hip, Leslie unlocked the back door and entered, the ubiquitous Fritz bounding up to her with unabashed ecstasy. After unsacking the purchases, she filled a caddy with cloths, brushes, cleanser and a squeegee, and began tackling the bathrooms. She had scrubbed and scoured her way into the hall when the doorbell rang and Fritz raced toward it in a barking frenzy.

Leslie pulled off her rubber gloves and went to the front door. The inquisitive next-door neighbor had come visiting, bearing a basket of freshly-baked muffins. Fritz had stopped the barking and was jumping joyfully.

"Hi. Welcome home, Leslie."

Before Leslie could express astonishment at the unexpected greeting, the woman extended a hand. "I'm Abigail Moffett. But just call me Abby." She glanced at the dog. "No, nothing for you, you adorable scamp."

Hugh's Abby. "Come in," Leslie invited, elated that a supposed rival was more grandmother than femme fatale. So Hugh had been aiding and abetting the green-eyed monster. At least in this instance.

"I don't want to stop you from your work. Hugh told me about your being here, though, and I wasn't about to wait around for him to introduce us."

"I'm not surprised that he hasn't. This is a temporary arrangement, you see."

"Oh?"

Leslie caught a look of unease as if Abby had supposed them reunited. Hugh's telling their neighbor about her being home was understandable. After all, it'd be impossible to keep the news a secret from someone in such close proximity. Apparently, however, he'd done a poor job of explaining how things really were.

"I imagine he'd prefer stashing me in the cellar—if the house had one—to introducing me around."

"Oh, how you do go on," Abby said, shaking her head. "From what I hear, he's delighted you're home."

What have you heard, Leslie almost asked aloud, but quickly regained her wits. *Abby's just being nice.* Leslie smiled graciously. "Sounds as though you've had experience in the diplomatic corps. Sure you won't come in for something to drink?"

"Give me a rain check and we'll get acquainted later." Abby reached for the door, then paused. "Why don't you come fishing with Hugh and me on Friday?"

"He'd have a fit."

"Then we won't give him any advance notice."

Leslie couldn't keep from laughing at the twinkle in Abby's eyes.

"You're a woman after my own heart."

"Then you'll come?"

"I just may at that."

*   *   *

Energized by Abby's brief visit, Leslie moved into high gear, getting a good start on cleaning the rest of the house. It was midafternoon and she was vacuuming the living room when Hugh walked in.

Sweeping a gaze across the room with its polished woods, gleaming glass tables and plumped cushions, Hugh's eyes came to rest on her disheveled appearance, then he thundered, "What in blazes are you doing?"

"What does it look like?" Leslie's eyes were wide with puzzlement, but her mind was working furiously. To begin with, it wasn't even three. Saturday was merely another workday for Hugh, and she hadn't expected him for hours. Second, Hugh was fastidious. He *liked* an orderly home. So why was he so put out over a little housework?

"You don't have to cook and clean for me," he complained, casting his briefcase into a handy chair. "You didn't before."

"So what's the big deal? Are you mad about today or about old yesterdays?"

Hugh paused thoughtfully, then held up his hands. "Forget I said anything. I didn't mean it to come across that way. It's only that you accused me of working too hard and now you're doing the same thing. I'm worried about you, Les. You don't look well. Lose a few more pounds and you could be hired out as a scarecrow."

"Gee, thanks."

"What happened to you in France?"

Disturbed by his question, Leslie deliberated on several flippant comebacks to lighten the tense atmosphere. That she'd been forced to eat her own cooking, that she'd endangered her health in a debauched lifestyle of wine, *men* and song, that she'd spent the whole year pining over him—which wouldn't have been all that flippant. The look of concern on his face, however, almost convinced Leslie to tell him the truth about her illness.

But the truth would invite more questions. Questions she wasn't prepared to discuss. Especially since the humiliating result was that she'd dragged herself home like a whipped animal. "Sorry I don't meet your exacting standards of beauty anymore."

"Quit being so damn smart-alecky and level with me. Have you been ill?"

"What's wrong, afraid you'll have to play nurse-maid?" she challenged. Raising a hand in oath, she said, "I solemnly promise I won't collapse on you." The hand dropped. "Frankly, I'm too beholden to you as it is to chance falling ill."

"So you plan to earn your keep around here by being a scrub woman? If the house isn't tidy enough for you, then call in a cleaning service."

"I can't pay for a cleaning service."

"I can."

"So why haven't you? If those gargantuan spider webs in the corners get any bigger, they'll be large enough to trap Fritz."

Hugh stole a glance toward the ceiling, then in spite of himself, started laughing. Leslie couldn't keep herself from joining in. "Son of a gun, did we always argue so much?" he said, shaking his head.

"I think we did," she said, resting a hip against the sofa.

"Maybe because the making up was so good." Suddenly, Hugh was cupping her elbows, pulling her up toward him, his eyes changing from amused to smoldering.

Leslie's eyes locked with his and her body involuntarily leaned into him. She wished he would kiss her the way she knew he wanted to. Instead, Hugh hesitated, seeming to weigh the situation in lawyerly fashion. His deliberation destroyed the moment, diffusing the feelings building between them. Leslie pulled away.

"I called the real estate company," she managed to say, in a tight little voice. "You were right about me needing to share the responsibility. An agent is coming by tomorrow and I wanted to have the house ready. That's why I was cleaning."

She expected him to be pleased she'd taken the initiative, but Hugh's scowl showed he was anything but. "You really are in a mad rush to sell."

"Well it *has* been a year, and as we both know, I need the cash."

"But at what cost? Are you going to kill yourself getting it? I can tell just by looking that you're beat."

"I am a little," she admitted.

"And I'll bet you worked right through lunch."

The way Hugh seesawed between chastising her and expressing concern over her well-being bemused Leslie. It implied that even if he no longer needed her, there was still some caring on his part. But how much or what it meant, she didn't know. It was hard not to let the possibilities get to her.

Composing herself, Leslie answered, "You lose that bet. Peanut butter and jelly sandwich. Apple. Glass of milk."

"I think we can do better than that for dinner. Why don't you rest while I trot next door and do a couple of chores for Abby, then we'll go out."

"Sounds good," she said, too tired to resist.

She showered and washed her hair, then took Hugh's suggestion and lay down. An hour later, she awoke to the sensation of him stroking her hair off her forehead, and then gently brushing the area with his lips. The tenderness of his touch evoked memories she'd been unable to subdue. Her hand moved up to catch his and she held it momentarily against her cheek.

"Feel better now?" he asked.

"Hmm," she murmured, wanting to draw him down beside her, wishing he'd take the initiative. The brotherly kiss on her forehead wasn't what she wanted—not even close.

"Then get up, lazy bones, and we'll go to dinner."

"A short detour," Hugh said, as he parked by the Neiman-Marcus entrance at Northpark Mall and shepherded her into the store.

"What for?"

"Some clothes that fit you. Everything you own bags. Just look at your reflection." He pointed at a full-length mirror and turned her sideways. "You could smuggle contraband in the seat of those slacks."

As if he had to tell me. "But I can't afford to shop here," Leslie protested. Just that morning she'd calculated her budget and the results were gloomy. Her only option for clothing was a discount store or resale place, if even that.

"We'll put it on my charge account."

"I won't accept anything more from you."

"Then consider it a loan. Let me do this, Les. You can pay me back later. When we sell the house, we'll take it out of your share. Okay?"

His words seemed reasonable. Yet Leslie knew that allowing Hugh to lend her money increased her obligation to him, in spite of what he said. Besides, there was something intensely personal about a man's buying you clothes. It bespoke a closeness that in their case was false.

Nevertheless, she meekly allowed herself to be led up the escalator to the women's wear department. Leslie tried on numerous garments, and at Hugh's insistence, presented all for his inspection. She sensed him assessing her along with the outfits, his gaze lingering entirely too long.

"That one flatters your figure," he'd say. And, "That shade of green's perfect with your hair."

She had to admit she did look snazzier in apparel that didn't hang in shroudlike folds. Being decked out in the latest fashion didn't hurt, either. She felt better about herself than she had in months.

"Don't change," he instructed Leslie after she performed a model's turn in a pair of brown linen trousers and matching sleeveless vest. "Wear it to the restaurant. Just clip off the price tag," he told the salesclerk.

Leslie might have declared that if Hugh could manage to underwrite these purchases, he could advance at least some of her portion of the house. She might have steadfastly refused the loan for the sake of principle. But at the moment, principle no longer seemed quite so important. Not if it meant pushing him away. As the clerk totaled the purchases, Leslie whispered to Hugh, "Thank you."

"Is that it—a simple thank-you? No complaints, no accusations?" His eyes had a twinkle, one that had been missing for ages. Leslie was elated at its reappearance.

"I thought you might appreciate a gracious acceptance for a change." She grinned at him. "Would you prefer a quarrel?"

"No, I rather like you this way. Even if I do realize that the peace won't last." His wry tone and teasing smile disconcerted Leslie to the very tips of her toes.

"Maybe I've quit arguing because it's no longer as much fun to make up," she said, deliberately reminding him of his earlier words.

"It could be fun," he retorted seductively, draping the plastic-covered clothing over one arm and squeezing her with the other. "You look irresistible right now."

"Flatterer."

They had dinner at a nearby restaurant. Leslie's wine cooler had a relaxing effect and tonight she saw a melting of their hostilities. "This is nice," she said, gesturing toward the strolling accordionist.

"Yes," Hugh agreed, saluting her with his wineglass. His knee touched hers, accidentally or on purpose, Leslie couldn't decide.

"Tell me about Paris. Was it what you hoped for?"

"In some ways," she answered cagily. "It's a beautiful city." Where was Hugh going with this topic? Perhaps she should find out. "Would you have missed me if I hadn't come back?" Her heart raced as she waited for his answer.

He responded by pulling her hand to his lips, his kiss across her fingertips lingering. The candlelight illuminated a tender message in his eyes. "Les—"

"Excuse me, sir. The lady has the scampi and you the pork loin. Right?"

The mood interrupted, Leslie's feelings of mellow optimism began to fade. She could well be reading too much into this. The thought caused her to furrow her brow.

"It's been a surprisingly nice evening," Hugh said, as though trying to recapture the earlier atmosphere.

He reached across the table to trace a fingertip across her knuckles. *Don't spoil it*, his gesture said.

Hugh could rest easy—being a spoiler was the farthest thing from her mind. Leslie found she was quite willing to hang on to the gentler mood. "Yes, it has been nice," she agreed.

It cut to the quick that after sharing more than one close moment, Hugh would toss her aside like yesterday's newspaper the minute they arrived home. He carried in her packages, fed Fritz, then reached for his car keys on the counter. "I forgot something at the office. I don't know how long I'll be."

Leslie didn't believe he'd forgotten anything, except maybe the fact he really didn't want to be with her. At the restaurant she had become positive that Hugh was signaling a thaw in their adversarial relationship. His cavalier desertion at a point when they should have been drawing even closer quickly set her straight. Tonight was benevolence on his part, pure and simple. Take the poor waif to dinner, get her some decent clothes, make her realize what she's been missing, then get rid of her.

He'd probably counted the minutes until he could rush off—to Grace's or Serena's or another girlfriend Leslie had yet to learn about.

After an hour of pacing and fuming, fuming and pacing, Leslie decided to test out her suspicions. She dialed the number of Hugh's office, holding her breath that he would answer and prove her wrong. If he was there, she would apologize for bothering him, then make excuses by saying that she had rung to thank him again for her new clothes.

When the phone continued to ring without answer, Leslie hung up, sadder and wiser. Her worst fears had been confirmed. Hugh hadn't gone back to work. He'd flown into the arms of some other woman. Leslie couldn't stem the tears that fell as feelings of foolishness took over. She should never have bought into such silly notions of reconciliation after a few short hours of togetherness. One evening could not fix a damaged relationship.

She didn't know when Hugh came in since she'd eventually cried herself to sleep. Fortunately he wasn't there to witness her red eyes the next morning. He was already up and out. Then again, for all she knew, he'd never come home at all.

CHAPTER FIVE

AFTER a late Sunday breakfast, Leslie set about with last minute preparations for the realtor's visit. She made the beds—both hers and Hugh's, which he hadn't bothered to straighten before he'd darted out— then proceeded to load the dishwasher and fix a fresh carafe of coffee. A candle was lit under a pot of liquid potpourri and flowers were brought in from the garden and arranged in vases throughout the house.

The realtor, Maggie Edwards, arrived promptly at one o'clock, stayed less than an hour, and left Leslie standing on the front steps with a set of instructions and some stern advice.

"These problems have developed since I was here last. You'll need to attend to them as soon as possible." She ripped off a page from a ruled tablet, handing it to Leslie before reiterating some of the items. "Replace that broken tile in the bathroom, get the windows washed inside and out, and have the carpets thoroughly cleaned." An accusatory glare was aimed at Fritz with the mention of the carpeting.

Leslie glanced at the rest of the page. A few more repairs, all minor. They didn't explain the house not selling. The realtor's next comments did.

"As I told your husband before, the asking price is completely out of line. A fair amount would be forty to fifty thousand less. If you really want to sell, I suggest you reduce your expectations to something more realistic. During the four months it's been listed, I've found it impossible to get anyone even to look

at your house. Talk to Mr. Campbell about renegoti-
ating, then give me a ring,'' she called, pausing in the
middle of the front walk en route to her car. ''Our
current agreement is expiring so we'll need to sign a
new one.''

Her mind spinning, Leslie watched as the black
Cadillac drove away and considered how much
weight to give to the realtor's comments. Hugh was
an astute businessman, some might say crafty. It
wasn't like him to stand on a price he knew to be
excessive.

Maybe Maggie Edwards didn't know what she was
talking about. Or maybe she wanted the price lowered
so the house would move quickly—along with her
commission. Then again, Hugh had confirmed the
lack of offers, and according to the realtor no one had
even looked at the house. Surely if the figure was in
line, someone would be looking, would be tendering
a bid, even a capricious one. And Ms. Edwards had
almost given the impression she wasn't interested in
representing them unless they agreed to come down
on the price.

Leslie spent the afternoon checking with other real
estate companies. While all expressed a need to see
the property before giving a firm appraisal, their initial
opinions were much the same as Maggie Edwards'—
the house was overpriced.

Leslie was taken aback at their pronouncements.
Not as much about the amount as about the why of
it. Hugh had never let on that he might have inflated
the asking figure. But then, Hugh had always loved
this place and there was no indication he'd changed
that opinion. Either he saw the value as higher than
anyone else did or he loved the property too much to
part with it, even though both of them could use the
money.

Leslie went to the kitchen to turn off the coffee-maker. She picked up an orange and was rolling it in her hands, more for something to do than because she planned to eat it. As she pondered over Hugh's motivations, the realtor's words pricked her consciousness. "Four-months listed," she'd said. *What about the other eight months?* No wonder nothing had happened. Hugh'd seen to that. When she heard his car, she dropped the orange back into the fruit bowl. The man was in for some heavy explaining.

He entered the kitchen, pulling a golf bag in after him and parking it by the door.

"First fishing, now golf. What next—polo?" she asked sassily, biding her time. Either Hugh had undergone a personality transplant, or he'd actually taken her concerns to heart. He still worked too hard, but work no longer consumed all his waking hours. "You're becoming a regular sportsman."

"A client introduced me to the game and I discovered I enjoy it," he said. "Besides, I make a lot of good contacts on the course."

"That sounds more like Hugh Campbell," she said. "I was beginning to wonder about you." Leslie picked up the orange again, feeling an even stronger need to keep her hands busy. "Something else I'm curious about. The realtor came by today and—"

"Should I start packing?" Hugh interrupted. "Have you sold my home out from under me?"

"No danger of that. Especially since the price you demanded is off the charts."

"I'm sure you fixed that real fast," he grumbled, opening the refrigerator and gazing inside. He pulled out a Sprite and popped the tab. Turning around, he said, "I was just trying to make sure we got full value."

"You were trying to make sure it didn't sell period. And you waited two-thirds of a year to make that feeble effort. Why, Hugh?"

He hesitated a moment before replying. "How was I to know you really wanted me to sell? You know how melodramatic you can be. I thought you'd get over being mad and come back after a few weeks. Or at least be home within a couple of months. I put it on the market after I realized that wasn't going to happen." He drank thirstily from the can.

His forthrightness threw her for a loop. "But eventually I did return," she said softly. "So what now?"

"That ought to be my line," Hugh said. "What now, Leslie?"

She didn't have an answer. The ringing of the phone bought her a reprieve as Hugh picked it up and spoke briefly.

"That was Phil Cotter—my golf partner. He called to reemphasize the fact that you are invited to a cocktail party at his house tonight. I guess he didn't trust me to carry through without his prodding. How about it?"

"I don't remember a Phil Cotter," she said, the conversation about the house pushed into the background.

"He's a doctor, an obstetrician. I represented him in a malpractice suit this year."

"You must have won if he's become a friend, as well as a client."

"As a matter of fact, yes, but it was a cakewalk—a ridiculous case that would have been funny if Phil's professional reputation hadn't been on the line. A woman sued him because her baby was three days overdue and he wouldn't induce labor.

"The child, a healthy one, I might add, was born

on the second of January, rather than the end of December and it cost the family a tax deduction for the previous year. She tried to claim mental anguish, but seeing it for what it was, the judge threw the case out. Everyone gripes about lawyers nowadays, then proceeds to sue at the drop of a hat.'' He grinned. ''Thank goodness, huh?''

''Keeps you in demand,'' Leslie agreed, her pique temporarily forgotten and her mood matching Hugh's good humor.

Hugh started out of the kitchen. ''I need a shower,'' he said, then stopped to prop a shoulder against the doorjamb. ''By the way, you haven't said whether you'd like to go to the cocktail party.''

''Do you want me to?''

''It's your decision,'' he answered noncommittally. Yet there was something about the way he looked at her and the way he stood, the casualness almost forced, that made her think it did matter to him. What Leslie wasn't sure of was why it mattered.

''Okay,'' she agreed nonchalantly, recognizing that now it was *her* casualness that was feigned. Her mind was running through a series of questions, questions she might never have the answers to unless she played out this hand.

According to Hugh, Phil had called to ensure she— Leslie—came to his party. Which meant she'd at least been mentioned to Hugh's friend. But in what context she had no clue. Had Hugh represented them as a couple, or was Phil Cotter merely curious about the runaway wife who was suddenly back on the scene? Leslie couldn't resist the opportunity to find out.

Whatever Phil's motivations, Hugh's were the ones that intrigued her more. As she started upstairs for her room, Leslie thought of the frothy new sundress from

Neiman-Marcus with its mid-thigh hem designed to reveal lots of leg. Hugh had prevailed upon her to buy it despite her objections that she'd have no place to wear such a showy number. Perhaps he'd known she'd need a party outfit when he insisted she get it.

"Hello, Leslie. Finally we meet. I'm Grace Cotter."

So Grace is Phil's wife. The woman greeting her was tall and lithe, her English rose complexion a contrast to her dramatic near-black eyes and a mane of shoulder-length brunette hair. As Hugh had said—and Grace's attire attested—definitely the silks and diamonds sort. She wore a halter-style jumpsuit of Thai silk and a multicareted tennis bracelet on her wrist. Her left hand bore more diamonds, showy wedding and engagement rings—rings pricey enough to be insured by Lloyds of London. Leslie cast Hugh a questioning glance.

"Leslie's wanted to meet you, too, Grace. She's been wondering about the lady who brought me home the other night."

"You should have joined us for dinner, Leslie. I would have insisted, but Hugh said you're were still fighting jet lag. Next time, though, I won't take no for an answer. How was France by the way?" Grace slipped an arm through Leslie's.

"Have you been there?" Leslie countered, hoping to avoid details yet wanting to appear friendly. Obviously, Hugh had been toying with her when discussing Grace earlier. His innuendos were designed to present Grace as a romantic interest, the same way he had originally alluded to Abby. And as with Abby, the innuendos were plainly a ruse. The woman next to her was entirely too accommodating to be a rival for Hugh's affections.

"Our last trip was several years ago when we spent a second honeymoon in Provence," Grace said. "Phil's schedule is as maddening as Hugh's. We seldom make it through a meal without him running off to the hospital, just as he did the other night when I brought Hugh home. I admire you for being independent enough to go abroad to work instead of sitting around waiting for your husband to come home. Being a translator, living abroad…it must have been exciting."

"Yes. Also lonely at times."

"But probably not as lonely for you as for Hugh. He sure was out of sorts without you." Grace patted his cheek solicitously and Leslie felt a secret satisfaction that their hostess was unwittingly exposing Hugh like this. He probably wanted to throttle Grace about now.

"Let me introduce you to our other guests while this guy of yours fetches us a drink," Grace said. "I'd like Perrier. Leslie?"

"I know what Leslie likes," Hugh growled as he started toward the bar, confirming her moment's old thought.

The party guests were strangers to Leslie and apparently new acquaintances of Hugh's. None of the stuffy crowd from TGT who always managed to intimidate Leslie with their uptight ways were there, thank heaven. She had always seen them as disapproving and was relieved Hugh had been forming new bonds and that the camaraderie was such that it extended to her, also.

Several people asked about her European tour. It became clear that, rather than admit she'd left him, Hugh had fabricated a cover story of a work and travel opportunity he'd insisted Leslie take advantage of. A self-serving explanation, but one which eliminated embarrassments tonight.

Whenever the questions about her long trip became too probing, Hugh's grip around her shoulders tightened, serving notice to Leslie not to betray his tale of domestic bliss. Leslie didn't mind covering for him. It was simpler for her, also. Besides, it gave her latitude to capitalize on a need to be close to him, a need that had gone unmet even though they shared a house.

She kept an arm wrapped possessively around his waist whenever he was standing near. Which was most of the time. He left her side only to refresh a drink. When others bid for his presence, he brought her along.

"Keep hanging on to your man," Grace muttered to Leslie as they joined Hugh, Phil and a trio of late arrivals who were chatting on the patio. Grace nodded toward a woman who was coming their way and whispered, "She's on the medical staff at Phil's hospital and has no respect for the sanctity of marriage. Recently she's set her sights on Hugh. I'm so glad you're here to keep those claws of hers retracted."

Leslie appreciated Grace's alert. She snuggled closer to Hugh as the predatory newcomer zeroed in, batting her eyelashes and flirting outrageously as if Leslie weren't plastered to his side.

Hugh appeared oblivious to the woman's interest. He maintained his hold around Leslie as he continued conversing with Phil and another of their golfing foursome. The public affection made Leslie feel secure...cherished. Even if the feelings were destined to be short-lived, she indulged herself. She hadn't experienced such affection from him in a long time.

The party began breaking up and Hugh and Leslie were among those taking their leave. "I like your friends," she said as they pulled away from the Cotters' sprawling Bent Tree home.

"Good. Maybe you'll hang around long enough to see them again."

Considering the chill in his tone, Hugh could have been addressing a hostile witness. Leslie wanted to kick herself for opening up and taking his attentions too literally. Every time she risked believing in their relationship, Hugh lashed out again.

His attitude was a complete turnaround now that the party mask had been discarded. This was the real Hugh. No promises, no assurances that he saw them as anything but two people having to live together because of difficult circumstances. And he was doing his damnedest to keep the difficulties alive. He just couldn't seem to get over his resentment about her leaving.

The car's air-conditioner vents were all directed at Hugh, so the frigid air couldn't be blamed for Leslie's shiver. Right now she felt as though that awful evening a year past had been reincarnated, that it would take only a couple of ill-advised words for a dangerous verbal battle to ensue.

Hugh's turning into their drive momentarily interrupted the unpleasant speculation. Once they were inside the house, however, Leslie knew she had to make a choice. She could utter a fast "good night" and rush upstairs like a coward or she could confront him. Confrontation won out. "Was all the husbandly devotion tonight merely for show, then?" Leslie's voice was purposely controlled, any hint that she was on the verge of tears hidden.

Hugh shrugged out of his sport coat, keeping his back to her. He hadn't anticipated this question. Actually, he'd thought Leslie would probably respond to his barb with a caustic one of her own. Then they could trade insults before one of them tired of the exchange and stomped off for the night. Good protection against his doing something stupid, like hauling her off to the bedroom.

So he'd resorted to a little subterfuge at the Cotters? So what? He hadn't wanted to be embarrassed in front of his friends—that's all—and besides, it felt good to act like old times. Was it a sin to want that? But that was then and now was now, and Hugh recognized he needed to bring things back under control. The gibe about her hanging around had been deliberate. As much for his own benefit as to taunt Leslie. He might want her back, but heaven only knew what Leslie wanted. She probably didn't know herself.

"Well, was it all show?" she asked again.

"I don't know," he answered, turning back toward her. Until she did know and could spell it out, he would continue to limit any tender moments between them. "I'd better check on Fritz." He started looking for the dog, determined to cut off any further probing from Leslie.

It was late Monday and Leslie's hips were braced against the bottom step of the swimming pool, the tepid water splashing against her shoulder blades. Fritz lay on the pool's deck, his shaggy black head hanging over the edge close to the surface, his nose meeting the top of the colored tile. Leslie slapped her hand in the water, sending a spray of droplets to shower the animal. Fritz jumped up and vigorously shook the water from his fur. Leslie laughed and splashed him again.

"You two having fun?"

Hugh. He'd left a note telling her not to expect him

until late. Since it was the first time he'd seen fit to advise her of his schedule, Leslie had interpreted the note as a positive sign. Still, she hadn't intended to be in the pool when he showed up. She'd been contemplating getting out for the past thirty minutes, but had put off making the move.

Now it was too late and she regretted being caught like this, wearing her old bikini. The suit which had formerly been a bit snug now fit looser but was no less revealing. If only her towel lay closer so she could cover herself when she came out of the water.

"Hard day?" he asked, his raised eyebrows underscoring the sarcasm.

"Not really. But tomorrow's my first day at work so I'll be putting in my final lap." She meant this as a hint for him to go away so she could climb out of the water without his perusal. She found it maddening that rather than taking the cue, Hugh just stood there like a spectator while she swam away from the shallow-end steps toward mid-pool.

"Must be nice to be a part-timer," he called out.

Leslie stopped swimming. "You should try it," she retorted. She was now at the opposite end of the pool, the deep end where she was treading water. She anchored her crossed arms on the rim and turned her back to him.

"Can't." Hugh walked around the pool perimeter until he was standing over her. "Some of us have to toil for a living, those of us destined to be ants. Only those—I won't name names—who are grasshopper material have the luxury."

She flipped her hair out of her eyes and glared up at him. *What was his problem tonight?* "Grasshopper, huh? Well, since ants are supposed to be strong little critters, why don't you flex one of your muscles and help me hop out of the pool?'' Her half-nakedness forgotten, she lifted a hand toward him.

"When did you become the helpless female?" he asked, grabbing the hand.

As their palms clasped, Leslie braced both feet against the side and jerked, catching Hugh by surprise and sending him flying past her into the water, only a "What the—?" coming before the splash.

He surfaced, hair matted on his head and his tie floating out in front of him. "I can't believe you did that. You're supposed to be an adult, remember?"

"I don't believe in acting adult more than twenty-three hours a day. Too bad you showed up at just the wrong hour."

"This happens to be a new suit I'm wearing. An expensive one."

"Well you ought to demand a refund—the material wrinkles." Leslie couldn't hold back a smile.

"My shoes are ruined, too."

"Yeah, I suspect they are. They don't make them like they used to."

"You think this is so cute, huh? Apologize...." He grabbed her head and pushed her under.

She came up laughing and sputtering. "How grumpy you are over a little dunking."

"Oh, yeah? We'll see about grumpy. Where's my apology?" He pushed her under again.

"Never," she sprayed out when resurfacing.

"Well I guess I'll have to drown you then." A third quick dunking.

"Okay, okay, I apologize," she spewed.

"Finally. And now for your next humiliation, we'll check out whether I can still go two laps for your one in a race."

"The odds are better tonight—your being in a wet business suit should give me an advantage."

"Oh, I don't plan to keep the suit on," he drawled. "In fact, I don't plan to keep much of anything on...." Hugh knew the words were provocative, but she'd started this and he wasn't about to let her challenge go unanswered. Despite his vow to keep their sexual attraction under control, keeping himself in check was impossible right now. He struggled out of his jacket and slapped it onto the pool deck. Next came his wing tips and socks, then the tie, the disrobing continuing all the way to black briefs.

When his fingertips reached for the band of the briefs, Leslie said, "Enough already. I'm going inside."

She could feel his eyes on every inch of her exposed skin as she climbed out of the pool and bent down for her towel. "Chicken," he jeered, gazing up at her.

Leslie hesitated only an instant. "You asked for it." She dropped the towel and dove back into the water.

At first it was harmless fun. The race, which he won, and after that a netless game of water volleyball, Fritz chasing around the pool deck, wanting to be part of the action. Hugh challenged her to a second race, which ended just like the other with his winning easily.

"Okay, I give," she said breathlessly, paddling to the side of the pool to get out. Hugh's arm around her waist kept her from leaving. "Still a chicken," he goaded.

"Oh, no, I'm a grasshopper, remember?" She twisted to face him.

"Whatever." He backed her against the edge,

pressing his body close to hers. "Damn, I missed you, Les." In the dappled tree-shaded light of the pool, his gray eyes were soft, their pupils enlarged. His hands cupped her face. "Please tell me...."

Leslie knew what he was asking and she couldn't deny him. "I missed you, too...it seemed like forever, I wanted—"

His lips on hers sealed any further explanation. They communicated instead with their passion, with their bodies. How they got from the pool to Hugh's bedroom was anybody's guess. Leslie didn't even want to think about it. To think would take away the magic, would give reality to the situation. She'd lain awake so many nights dreaming of Hugh, of being in his arms. Now that her dreams had taken shape, she refused to ruin the moment or deny herself this opportunity.

It was early morning when she awakened. Leslie could see a light from beneath the door of the adjoining bathroom and could hear the hum of a hair-dryer. The door opened and Hugh came into view, wearing only his underwear. He went to the closet and pulled a white shirt from off the hanger. She watched him dress, unsure whether he was aware of his audience as he tucked the shirt into gray suit trousers. The room seemed eerily quiet, even the rasp of his zipper audible. Leslie longed for him to forget the clothes and come back to bed with her.

Draping a silk jacquard tie around his neck, he crossed the room and sat on the edge of the bed. "You're awake," he said.

She nodded and smiled, the smile dying on her lips as she glimpsed his foreboding expression. Words weren't necessary to say that he was having second thoughts about their lovemaking.

Nevertheless, he did use words. "I'm not sure how to say this. 'I'm sorry' isn't right, because frankly I enjoyed every minute of it. But what happened shouldn't have—we both know that."

Hugh rubbed a hand across his freshly-shaven chin as he stared out the window into the gray dawn. *Why the hell couldn't I keep my hands off her? Why does my gut ache with wanting her now?* Leslie had given him no assurance she planned to stay. Fact was, she'd given him *every* reason to believe she'd trot off again the instant she had the means to—which could be to-morrow if the house sold. Or it might be months from now. If he'd barely managed to restrain himself for a week, then how in blazes was he going to subdue his raging hormones if it did take months?

"Hugh...." Leslie reached toward him. "*Was* it merely a lapse?" He knew too clearly what she meant. She was asking him to admit he was still nuts about her. But he wouldn't, not yet. He'd made all the admission he intended to in that bed with her.

The signals told him she'd welcome him back be-tween the sheets right now. He almost moaned aloud at the idea. Spending the morning in bed, calling the office to cancel his appointments...no, he had to work and so did she.

Get a grip, fella. Taking her up on her unspoken offer would be crazy. Once he let himself go again, he'd be up to his eyeballs in emotional quicksand. He had to avoid it—he couldn't handle loving her and losing her again.

He caught her hands and squeezed them, then quickly released them. He must get out of here. "I need to run," he said, hating himself for the coward he was. He crossed over to the dresser and began wrapping his tie into a Windsor knot. "What happened may have been inevitable," he said, his back to Leslie, "but yes, it was definitely a wrong move for two people with their own lives to live. Let's not read any more into this than necessary. We just gave in to our lusts, that's all."

The flash in her eyes reflected in the mirror showed the message had hit home—just as he had known it would. He felt her anguish, wishing he didn't have to say and do these things, but avoidance and shock therapy were the name of the game if he was to survive.

Leslie sat up, hugging the sheet to her chest. "Well, don't worry," she said, her eyes narrowed to slits. "I guarantee you there'll be no repeats of last night."

Her acerbic response was exactly what he'd wanted to provoke, what was needed to keep this dangerous situation under control. Nevertheless, the pronouncement irritated him more than he could have imagined. So much so that he couldn't hold his tongue. Leslie wasn't going to have the last word here. "Good luck on that guarantee," he scoffed, turning to face her. "But if you weaken, I promise not to hold you to it. Let's face facts, we're a combustible combination, easily ignitable."

"Maybe so, but I'll make sure I have a fire extinguisher handy from now on. Our marriage is over. There's no need to make matters any worse than they already are."

Hugh grabbed his suit jacket from the closet and threw open the door. "We'll see. Have a good day at work, Les," he said as he left.

Leslie grabbed a pillow and flung it toward the door just as Hugh shut it behind him. Damn him. Their lovemaking had been special to her, had given her renewed hope. Now Hugh was demeaning it as nothing more than a case of simple lust. Sure there was lust, but her feelings were real, a natural outpouring of the love she still held for him.

Hugh, on the other hand, was admittedly taking advantage of a handy bed partner. A bed partner he assumed would be ready and willing anytime he lit the fuse. Well, maybe she was the one who'd started things yesterday by impulsively pulling him into the pool, but it wasn't going to happen again. He was in for a big surprise the next time he expected fireworks in the bedroom.

Up to now, she'd made a diligent effort to keep their relationship platonic, to make this living arrangement as comfortable as possible under the circumstances. Now all bets were off. Leslie was going to be a regular temptress from now on, do everything she could to entice Hugh, then—once he was so sure her ''guarantee'' was faltering, she'd tell him a cold shower was the best he could hope for. That would take him down a peg or two…and provide her a sweet taste of the revenge she now desperately sought.

''Oh, right,'' Leslie said aloud. Vamping Hugh with the intent to rebuff him was really a smart plan. About the same sort of kamikaze mission as taking off for Europe on the spur of the moment. Hugh was right about their spontaneous combustion. If she had any doubts about that, last night should have put them to rest. Climbing Mount Everest in open-toed sandals was as achievable as her being able to refuse making love with Hugh once their libidos were aroused.

What she needed to do—what she had to do—was ensure they never again reached that point of no return. Hugh had certainly offered no argument about their marriage being over. She needed to be armor-plating her heart, not exposing it to more danger. Surely there was some other way to get even.

CHAPTER SIX

LESLIE dragged herself out of bed and went into the master bath. A gentle pummeling in the large whirlpool tub would be just the thing to rev her up for this workday. First the body, then the mind. It didn't help that Hugh's aftershave still lingered in the air or that his wet clothes, now hanging on the towel rod, brought back images of last night.

The suit had already started to shrink. *Serves him right.* "He deserves more than a shrunken suit, he deserves to…to…I'll think of something," she told Fritz through the open door as he gnawed on a tattered chew-toy.

Back in her own room, she dressed quickly, determined to push away errant thoughts of that hurtful skirmish with Hugh. *Going to work, having something to do will be my salvation.* Last week, she'd had the opportunity for only the briefest exchanges with old office colleagues. Getting reacquainted, and being on the road to autonomy again, should help soothe her troubled psyche.

Even though she arrived thirty minutes early, Bert Byers was already there. "Good morning," she said.

He glanced at the wall clock. "Having you show up on time would be shocker enough. But early…." He clutched his chest.

"I've turned over a new leaf. Lots of new leaves, in fact."

"Punctuality's good, but don't change too much,

kiddo," he said affectionately, ushering her into his office and closing the door. Pastries and a carafe of coffee waited on a tray. He poured them both a cup of coffee, then foisted a blueberry muffin on Leslie and demanded that she eat it while they talked.

"Now that you're on the payroll," he began, "I feel I have some rights to be an official buttinski."

"Should I have my attorney present before the interrogation starts?"

"*Your attorney* is just the person who should be present, only I'm guessing you weren't referring to Hugh, simply trying to smart talk your way out of this. I want some answers. Like I said last time, you don't look so good—way too scrawny."

"Not scrawny. My figure is called svelte. Sort of like Julia Roberts."

"Right," he said. "And I'm sort of like Sean Connery."

Leslie glanced at his ample girth and laughed.

"Okay, Marlon Brando then." She laughed louder. Bert laughed, too, but he was not letting a bit of levity deter him. "Now start explaining or we're going to be here all day."

That determined gleam in his eyes said she'd better tell all or else. Leslie sent up a silent prayer, asking to be spared this confessional.

As though in answer, Bert's telephone rang. "Well hello, Hugh. Funny you should call just now, 'cause I happen to have your better half in my office. She's on time and looking great. Here, I'll let you talk to her." Ignoring Leslie who was vigorously shaking her head "no," he thrust the receiver at her.

Defiantly, Leslie refused to take it, instead grabbing a big piece of muffin, intent on shoving it into her mouth and rendering herself unable to speak. A glare from Bert stopped her and Leslie reluctantly dropped the muffin on a napkin and took the phone. "Hello," she said warily.

She could hear Hugh clearing his throat. "How are you doing?"

Leslie managed to curb the response she wanted to give. Bert was sitting less than three feet away, unabashedly eavesdropping. "Why I'm just terrific," she said. "Thanks for asking."

He cleared his throat again. "Actually, I just called to check with Bert on his will."

"Oh?" Leslie knew she should feel grateful for the reprieve. Hugh didn't want to talk to her any more than she wanted to talk to him. "Then I'll let you get back to Bert." Leslie passed the receiver back across the desk, a forced smile plastered on her face.

She half listened as Bert and Hugh continued their conversation, at the same time trying to come to terms with why she felt even more miserable than before. *What did you expect—an apology? How easily you forget. Hugh's never been big on apologies.*

Eventually Bert hung up, shifting his attentions back to Leslie. "When are you going to cut that guy some slack?"

"Pardon me?"

"That phone call said it loud and clear. Hugh is bonkers over you and I think you're being too hard on him."

"The phone call was about *your* will."

"My will doesn't need updating. That was just a ruse to check on you."

"Oh, pulleeze, Bert."

"Couples have disagreements."

"You don't know the half of it."

"Right, like I haven't been married for thirty-nine years."

"Can we talk about something else?"

"Okay." Bert picked up his coffee cup, slowly savoring a sip before putting it down again. "How about leveling with me, then. What's wrong with you? Physically, I mean. Mentally, I already know your head's screwed on crooked."

"I suppose you'll hound me until I tell you."

Bert nodded.

Leslie leaned in closer, not wanting her words to travel past the boundaries of the office. "I was sick for a while. Nothing major. Hepatitis A and a couple of complications thrown in."

"I'd say that's pretty major. So how are you doing now?"

"Maybe not one hundred percent recovered, but on the mend. Except for some antibiotics I'm taking for a sinus infection and some vitamins to build me up, I'm nearly off medication...definitely well enough to work. But if you'd feel better, I'll get a medical release."

"Nonsense. You don't have to do that. Long as you're okay. I wouldn't want to be responsible for a relapse."

"I'm okay. And Bert...?"

"Yeah?"

"Don't tell anyone about the hepatitis. I wouldn't want people to think I'm contagious. If anyone asks—"

"They'll ask, believe me. How do you intend to explain away your pallor and weight loss? A bad case of turista?"

"That's as good as anything."

"For here, maybe so. But what about Hugh? Why

haven't you told him? And don't say you have. We're friends and we talk. He'd have mentioned something this serious. What's going on with you two?''

''It's a long story, too long to go into now when I have a day's work staring me in the face. You do have some stuff ready for me, right?''

Bert nodded resignedly. He shuffled through a stack of papers on his desk and pulled out a manila folder. ''See what you can do with these.''

Leslie took the folder and started to leave, pausing at the door to turn back to Bert. ''I don't suppose there's any point in my asking you not to tell Hugh about the hepatitis, is there?''

''Out of deference to your weakened condition?''

Leslie knew Bert's qualified response was a sure sign he'd blab the minute he had a chance. While she adored Bert Byers, she'd also be the first to classify him as a notorious meddler. He probably should have gone into social work inasmuch as he liked nothing better than being Mr. Fixit with other people's problems. An abundance of caring was what drove him, but sometimes she wished he would live and let live. She probably should have been more discreet with him.

But it was too late for discretion. As fast as his pudgy fingers could push the phone buttons to Hugh's office, Bert would be calling Hugh back.

''I talked to Bert later today,'' Hugh announced, walking out into the backyard where Leslie was reading the newspaper and drinking a carton of apple juice. Not even a hello, or a pat to Fritz, before he started in.

''Oh, and what did he have to say?'' she asked,

carefully folding away the paper, determined to remain unruffled.

"You know damn well what he said." Hugh's voice rose and his face began coloring. "Why didn't you tell *me* about the hepatitis? Months ago. I'd have jumped on the next plane to France if I'd had any idea you needed me."

Foolish man. He's never realized how much I need him. "I didn't want to interfere with your work."

"Work be damned! I'd have been there in an instant if I'd known what was going on. I can't believe all the visions I had of you romping through the French countryside with charming Frenchmen at your side, and then to find out…the least you could have done was tell me about it when you got back—especially when I asked whether you'd been sick. Or did you think Bert could lay on a better guilt trip? I felt like a seventh grader being chewed out by the principal when he unloaded on me. Called me an idiot and an insensitive clod in the same sentence."

"I did plan to tell you myself," she said defensively, not feeling particularly sympathetic considering Hugh's gauche treatment of her that morning.

"Oh, and when would that have been? After you'd finished alerting the rest of Dallas?"

Leslie was disturbed by his anger and the hurt in his voice, but angry herself, in fact twice as mad as she'd been before. Just like a man to tromp all over a woman's feelings, then cry foul when he felt mistreated.

"I was getting around to it," she snapped.

"Damned slowly, I'd say. So it's easier to talk to your boss than your husband?"

"Sometimes it is," she said, with a little less conviction. "I had no intention of sharing the information with Bert, either, but you know how he is. The man cons you and bullies you into saying things you shouldn't. I asked him not to rush to you with the message, but frankly, once he knew, I expected him to do just what he did.''

''You could have called my office and beaten him to the punch.''

''Sure. I'm going to spend my first day of a part-time job on personal phone calls. Why are you so bothered? Didn't you make it quite clear this morning after we finished sating our 'lust' that our lives are on separate paths, that our marriage is over? You didn't particularly come across as a man who'd be concerned over a little illness.''

''There you go again, twisting my words. I believe you're the one who pronounced the marriage over. Accepting the inevitable doesn't mean I'm some callous lout who wouldn't be distressed about your being ill.''

He seemed pretty callous to her right now, dismissing last night's lovemaking the way he had and acting like the end of their marriage was just a little road bump in his life. ''It's not concern for me that's bothering you,'' Leslie charged. ''It's your image you're worried about. You're anxious about the way things might appear to Bert—and to others.''

''Is that the reason I spent half the afternoon at the library and on the phone with Phil researching hepatitis?''

''That was unnecessary. You could have asked me and I'd have told you all you need to know.''

''Past experience said your information sharing's not particularly reliable.''

Leslie ground her teeth in aggravation. ''So what did you find out, *Doctor* Campbell?''

"I found out," he said, easing into a patio chair and leaning forward, elbows resting on his knees, "that there's an alphabet of hepatitises or hepatiti... whatever...A, B, C...and that type A—the kind you had—is not as severe as B and C, thank goodness. I was told that it's spread through contaminated food or water and that there's greater risk for people in parts of the world where hygiene is poor.

"The incubation period is three to six weeks and in some cases there is no illness. In others, there are flulike symptoms and jaundice, which is usually mild. Have I described your situation?"

"Pretty much."

"Good." He leaned back and targeted his gaze on her, his eyes like twin lasers. "Then if you'll answer a couple of questions, I can complete my case study."

"Fire away." *You can't intimidate me any more than you already have.*

"Do you know how you got it?"

"Not really. Maybe at a restaurant. And apparently here in the U.S. I started feeling bad soon after I got to Paris. And your next question?" Her stare was equally as penetrating as Hugh's.

"Are you okay now? You should have recovered a lot faster than you have. Why did it take so long?"

"Well, every case is different," she hedged, "but part of it was my own fault. You know how I've never been sick. When the symptoms began, I just blamed them on a travel bug and figured I'd shake it off. So I put off going to the doctor and raced around sight-seeing instead."

Despite the obvious strain on Hugh's face, that was all the explanation he deserved or was going to get. Leslie wasn't about to tell him that she'd delayed seeking medical attention because she'd attributed the weakness and malaise to an illness of the heart—to missing him. That because of the delay, recovery had been much more drawn out.

"But I'm perfectly fine now," she hastened to add. "I'll soon be counting calories again and having the energy of a five-year-old. Speaking of calories," she said, more than ready to end the discussion, "I was going to start my dinner. Shall I cook enough for two?"

"No thanks. I have an engagement this evening."

"But of course, why should this night be different from any other?" she sniped. "Then I'll get on with my lamb chop and you can get on with...with your engagement."

A sly grin played across Hugh's lips, then quickly disappeared, as though it had come and gone of its own volition. "By the way," he said, now somber, "we're having dinner with Bert and Molly Thursday. I couldn't get out of it." His tone indicated he'd as soon dive headfirst into a tar pit as go.

"Oh, how awful. That means you'll have to endure my company for a whole evening."

"What I don't want to endure is an evening of marital combat in front of our friends."

"I have no intention of being a combative guest and making Molly miserable," Leslie said defensively. She sighed wistfully. "Gee I've missed her." Molly Byers was an old-fashioned homemaker, whose house always smelled of heavenly kitchen aromas, who always wore an apron and who lovingly abused all her friends with crushing embraces and too much good food.

Leslie *had* missed her, perhaps more than anyone else in Dallas other than Hugh and Bert. Too bad Hugh had to be part of the invitation. It could be a delightful evening otherwise. The thing to do was keep it a simple visit with old friends and steer clear of any discussion of future plans.

Leslie didn't see Hugh the next morning. She was awakened by Bert around eight-thirty, with an appeal that she come into the office. He'd set up an eleven o'clock conference call with an Argentine firm and thought a translator might be required. The fact of her services being needed was gratifying. Now she didn't feel she'd tramped quite as hard on Bert Byers's good nature by asking him to take her back.

As she dressed and ate breakfast, there was evidence that Hugh had come home at some point. A pile of spilled coffee grounds, a half-filled carafe of coffee and an empty cup littered the kitchen cabinet.

The small mess somehow intrigued Leslie. It bespoke a gentler Hugh, more relaxed, less a perfectionist. Only now and then did he regress into his old obsessive-compulsive self, the man whose shoes were lined in a straight row in his closet and the one who couldn't resist alphabetizing the canned goods in the pantry.

Maybe her leaving had affected him almost as strongly as it had her. Sure it'd made him mad—the hostility was almost pulsating at times. But had these changes she was now witnessing resulted from the trauma of her departure, also? She thought they had. Too bad Hugh couldn't have mellowed a year ago and given her some hope for their marriage. Instead, in those last days before she'd left for France, hope had drained out of her body as if through a sieve. And, these changes in Hugh notwithstanding, events of the last twenty-four hours had not restored an ounce of that hope.

*   *   *

Abby was already watering her flowers when Leslie backed out of the driveway headed for work. The older woman waved, then dropped the hose and came over to the curb. Leslie stopped the car and rolled down the window.

"You are coming to the lake with us Friday, aren't you?" Abby asked.

Truth be told, Leslie had forgotten the invitation. On the verge of declining, she stopped and reconsidered. She was by nature open to new experiences and what a divine way to irritate the heck out of Hugh. Just what she might be looking for as retribution. "I don't know a thing about fishing, but I'm game," she said to Abby.

"Hugh leaves the office at noon and I pack a picnic lunch so we can get away as soon as he changes. Be ready around one."

That decision made, Leslie felt better. Intruding on Hugh's fishing might not be a knockout punch as far as revenge, but at least it was something to show him he didn't hold all the cards. Being more in control was revitalizing. Work today, plus the knowledge that there was plenty to keep her busy tomorrow on her regular Thursday schedule also helped, and added to her feeling of empowerment. Maybe business would improve to the point where she'd be able to resume her full-time regimen at Byers Textiles.

When she arrived home that afternoon there was no sign of Hugh. Only Fritz, who greeted her enthusiastically. "Hi, boy," she said, picking up the gyrating bundle of fur. "He may be neglecting us, but we won't let him get away with it, will we?" Fritz licked her cheek, evoking a giggle. "Wait till he finds out about his new fishing buddy."

Leslie had spent a lot of the day thinking about the

fishing excursion and had begun to view it more and more as an opportunity. A whole afternoon to bedevil Hugh and with a witness present where he couldn't fight back. She now had a clear mission.

So engrossed was she in her plans that she almost failed to see the blinking red light on the answering machine, a smug communication from Serena that Hugh had left town on a business trip. He hadn't even bothered to make the call himself. Worse, he hadn't passed on any indication of where he was going or when he'd be back. Was she about to be stood up for dinner at the Byerses' tomorrow? Was he going to score with more humiliation before she even got her chance at bat?

Leslie was still brooding the next afternoon when she received another call from Serena telling her Hugh's plane would be late, but that he'd meet her at the Byerses'. She should be grateful he was coming, but Leslie felt a niggling disappointment that Hugh couldn't be bothered with stopping by the house first so they could go together. It wouldn't have delayed him by more than ten or fifteen minutes.

The message was clear—he was avoiding spending a smidgen more time than was necessary with her and he preferred the peace of driving to Bert and Molly's without her by his side.

"My goodness gracious, you are a mite of a girl now, just like Bert said." Molly Byers relieved her of a bouquet of multicolored roses and placed them on the table in the foyer, then wrapped Leslie in a hug. "They're lovely. From the garden?"

Leslie nodded and set her clutch purse beside the roses.

"Hugh arrived a minute ago," Molly said, a hand

on Leslie's forearm. "He's been telling us how you're both trying to mend things. Nothing could make us prouder. Marriage is tough sometimes." Molly turned to pick up the roses. "I should know," she said with a laugh. "I've put up with Bert Byers almost forty years." She sniffed the bouquet. "But it's worth it, Leslie. I can promise you that."

The words spoken, Molly gave a little titter. "Don't tell Bert I've been blabbing so. He made me promise not to interfere."

Leslie smiled in return. Obviously Bert thought interfering was his sole prerogative.

"The guys are in the family room mixing a pitcher of strawberry daiquiris. Shall we join them?"

Leslie nervously patted her hair as she followed Molly through the house. She'd worn the floral sundress again and had swept her auburn hair into a careless knot, with a couple of escaping tendrils to soften the look. It was a fussier style than she usually favored and she hoped to capture notice without drawing attention to the fact she'd gone to extra trouble.

Leslie knew exactly why it was so important she look good tonight. She'd attempted using the excuse that the effort was for Bert and Molly, but truth be told it had been in hopes of impressing Hugh. *Eat your heart out*, was what she wanted to say.

And impressed Hugh seemed—to those who didn't know better—as he rushed across the room to drape his arm around her and kiss her soundly. "Hi, sweetheart," he said, acting overjoyed to see her again. "Don't you look beautiful."

"Hello, darling," she responded, equally as insincerely. Apparently his pride dictated pretense in front of Bert and Molly, just as it had at the Cotters'. Well, she had a bit of acting talent, too. "I didn't expect you to beat me here," she chirped, "what with your plane behind schedule. How was your trip? Did you nail down a new client?" Leslie hadn't the foggiest notion where he'd gone or why, but if it wasn't law-firm business, then Hugh deserved the embarrassment she would create for him. She entwined her fingers with his and they walked together to the bar where Bert was filling stemmed glasses with the frozen pink drink.

"I was just telling Bert that it promises to be a tough case," Hugh said. "A leasing dispute between two oil companies. Both sides are pretty entrenched so I doubt we'll manage any kind of settlement out of court."

They perched on barstools, Leslie's high-heel sandals—a fashion look she normally eschewed—hooked on the rung of her stool. Molly placed a vase filled with the roses on an end table, then joined Bert behind the bar and initiated a toast. "To Leslie and Hugh. Together again."

"Hear, hear," Bert chimed in, raising his glass.

Hugh was smiling but his eyes were emitting a warning to Leslie as he acknowledged the toast. Leslie already realized she had no choice but to go along. However, she wasn't about to cave in entirely to the happy-ever-after routine; as glasses lifted, she added, deliberately reminding Hugh of his days-old remark, "And to combustible combinations."

Bert and Molly looked confused.

Hugh arched an eyebrow. "Sorry, private joke," he said lamely, wrapping an arm around Leslie and brushing her cheek with a kiss. "Cool it," he murmured.

Leslie gave a weak smile in return and took a welcome swallow of the daiquiri. Dinner and the rest of the evening promised to be torturous. Hugh's public actions were a total contrast to those private signals he was issuing. On the surface, he was being as solicitous as a brand new husband, constantly seeing to her needs, asking her opinions, touching her.

For a while, Leslie was so addled by his attentions, she had difficulty choking down her prime rib. She only managed to keep eating because everyone at the table seemed to be watching. Hugh, wary that she might say too much, and Bert and Molly either maintaining a health watch or beaming like proud parents with their two wayward children back in the fold.

As expected, Molly, queen of her kitchen, refused their offers to help clear the table or load the dishwasher. She and Bert ushered them into the living room for coffee and dessert—a rich chocolate torte.

There were second cups of coffee and more conversation, and during much of this time Hugh's fingers were laced with Leslie's, the back of her wrist lying on his muscular thigh. He didn't even loosen his grip as he raised both their hands to check his watch. "This has been great," he said, "but we'd better be running along." Taking a last sip of coffee, he returned the china cup to its saucer and stood. Leslie got up, also.

"It's been such a treat having you two over again," Molly said, linking arms with Hugh and Leslie as she walked between them to the door. "And, Leslie, I'm so glad you're back." Molly's eyes misted as she spoke and Leslie felt a stab of remorse at the charade they had perpetrated at the expense of the well-meaning Byers. How many more individuals were to be treated to this game of "Let's Pretend"? How many friends were going to be let down when the sham was revealed? Too many.

After a round of goodbye pecks on the cheek, Leslie and Hugh exited out into the night and started for their respective cars. The evening had been pleasant—some of it anyway—the sort of time they'd shared before Hugh's work consumed every waking hour.

It wasn't that Leslie had demanded nonstop parties and entertainment. She'd just wanted to be with her husband and occasionally with people who were important to both of them. Why had Hugh never understood that? Did he finally have a clue?

Leslie's expectation of enlightenment on Hugh's part was quickly crushed. "I need to run by the office," he said. "Haven't any idea how long I'll be, so don't wait up for me."

"I wouldn't think of it," she said, her tone purposely syrupy. "However, I have a couple of questions before you run off."

He leaned against the car fender. "Shoot."

"I'd love to," she responded. "But a prison cell isn't my cup of tea. Why in the world did you tell Bert and Molly we're patching things up?"

"What did you want me to tell them—that you're secretly plotting your next getaway?"

"While you're the perfect, devoted husband—one who sprints off to work the instant he returns from a business trip."

"I've been back four whole hours. I thought you were upset I'd misled Bert and Molly." He took a step toward her. "Sounds like your real gripe is that I'm not following you home."

"In your dreams," Leslie said defensively. "What's wrong, Hugh, are you escaping to the office because you're afraid I misread those showy romantic overtures in front of Bert and Molly? That I saw them as a promise of things to come? Is it easier to dodge me than spend time with me?''

''What makes you think that?'' he retorted, almost too quickly. Leslie was reading him too well. He did feel a need to get away, and stay away. If Leslie only knew what a number she did on him, how she up-ended his equilibrium and skewed all his thought processes. She was right. He was a coward. It was pathetic.

''Perhaps you're afraid of a recurrence of Monday's...ah, performance,'' she continued taunting. ''Scared I'll be lying in wait in the pool for you when you get home. Cause you to lose your head like you did the other night.''

This was stupid. Leslie knew she'd never win by trying to turn the tables on Hugh, a man professionally trained to make verbal mincemeat of opponents. But now that her mouth was in gear she couldn't seem to stop herself. Her hurt pride was propelling her.

''You sound as immature as ever,'' he replied tersely, afraid she could see the caring lying right below the surface. If Leslie were a bit more perceptive, she'd realize he'd irrevocably lost his head, his heart, the very first day he met her, never to regain them. Trading slight for slight seemed the only way to maintain even a semblance of control and keep his self-respect. ''I thought you'd grown up a little.''

Leslie slumped against the car door, wishing she'd left well enough alone, instead of setting herself up for more hurt. She glanced past Hugh toward the house. The two Byerses were standing at the window, watching the exchange. ''We have an audience,'' she murmured.

Hugh turned. ''They care about us.'' His tone was now softer, penitent. He propped a hand against the car and pulled her toward him with the other. "It's best if they think we've merely been lingering to chat," he whispered conspiratorially. Then, without any warning, his lips met hers. The kiss went on for what seemed an eternity, but to Leslie still ended all too soon. He walked her around to the driver's side and helped her inside the car. Good thing he did, for her knees were wobbly. "See you later," he said and disappeared behind the tinted windows of his van.

As she drove away with the kiss consuming her thoughts, Leslie reminded herself that Hugh had done it to her again, made her prey to her own emotions. That embrace and kiss were intended only for the Byerses' benefit. It was dumb, dumb, dumb for her to have responded. Obviously she'd never learn. She did this to herself repeatedly, only to be disappointed. Hugh Campbell would never change. He didn't even want to.

CHAPTER SEVEN

OR DID HE, Leslie thought, home now and preparing for bed. Having learned so much about herself in that year away from Hugh, she shouldn't dismiss the possibility that Hugh had used the time for introspection, as well. Leslie wished they could talk about all that had happened between them. Talk honestly and openly, without the incessant one-upmanship that dominated every discussion.

In all fairness, the longer she was around Hugh, the more she could see he *was* different, more relaxed, less driven. And the more she observed, the more convinced Leslie was that the changes weren't simply superficial. Even with Hugh's frequent disappearing acts, they'd spent more actual time in each other's company these past ten days than they had in the three months before she'd left for France.

And he'd held on to the house. A link with her, a stronger link now that she was sharing it—*at Hugh's suggestion*. All of that said something, too.

Hugh's demeanor now seemed to attest to a desire for life to be more balanced. Maybe there was still some hope for them—for a reconciliation—after all. If Hugh wanted one. That was the unknown factor.

The flash of lights in the darkened bedroom and Fritz's sleepy, halfhearted attempt at a bark told her Hugh was home. It was little more than an hour since she'd arrived herself. In the silence of night, Leslie could hear the door unlocking, then the muffled laughter of a late talk show on television, the rumble of the ice-maker releasing cubes into a glass, followed by the television being clicked off. When his footfalls sounded on the stairs, she kicked off the sheet. Oh, no. Hugh wasn't going to get away with sneaking to his room.

"Hello." She greeted him at the top of the stairs, feigning what she hoped was a casual pose even though her heart was pounding like a jackhammer. Luckily there were no sound effects to give it away.

"I thought you'd be asleep by now. You've had a long day," he said.

"So have you."

"I'm not convalescing."

"Neither am I. I feel more energetic than I have in ages." It was true. A few months ago she wouldn't have been able to work even half a day, much less put in a full eight hours and then go out for the evening. Today she hadn't even thought about her illness. Being with Hugh was proving to be a surprisingly effective antidote against dwelling on her health.

His tie already loosened, now he was undoing the knot and tugging until the tie slithered free from the collar. He held the length of silk and waited, as if poised for Leslie's next move. "You didn't stay long at the office," she said.

He shrugged indifferently, but the intensity in his eyes was anything but indifferent. "I couldn't keep my mind on the brief I was drafting." He didn't even attempt to hide his interest, his head moving as he examined her from head to toe.

Leslie's attire wasn't particularly seductive—a lavender cotton nightshirt—but Hugh knew as well as she that beneath that cotton was bare skin, skin he'd recently spent an entire night getting reacquainted with.

"We need to talk," she said huskily, becoming aware of a sexual tension building between them.

"What's on your mind?" he asked. "More complaints?"

"No."

"You mean you really just want to talk? Sure you're not looking for something else?" He rubbed the side of his neck as he leaned against the top newel of the stairs. "Unless this is a come-on, Les, I suggest you scurry back to your room. And lock the door behind you."

"There's no come-on." Leslie'd placed herself in a vulnerable situation, but she wasn't going to run, nor to back down. "And no lock, for that matter."

"Then ram a chair under the knob," he snarled, brushing past her on the way to his bedroom.

"Why are you so threatened by me, so afraid to be around me?" she called after him, feeling a surge of power. "Maybe you should be the one to lock your door...to keep your bedroom sacrosanct."

He wheeled around. "Join me there whenever you like. Say in ten minutes? Just let me grab a quick shower and we can have that..." He smirked. "'Talk.'"

A long pause.

"No?" he said. "Well, another time." He continued to his room and shut the door.

Confused, Leslie trudged to her own room. *What did I hope to gain with that scenario?* All she'd wanted tonight was some honest conversation to get everything out in the open and he'd treated her like a wanton woman. The man was always leaping to conclusions; there wasn't a shred of—

Leslie stopped. *If conversation was all you wanted, then why wait for him up here? You could have gone downstairs. You also could have put on a robe.* The wave of heat traversing through her body left her feeling incongruently cold. She'd spoken one way and acted another and he had called her bluff. But she wasn't going to let him get away with it.

Slipping into a terry robe, she secured the sash tightly around her. Then she stormed down to Hugh's room.

Hugh, sitting on the side of the bed and removing his wristwatch, looked up. "So you're taking me up on the offer." He set the watch on the bedside table.

"No, I'm not, not the offer you're referring to anyway. I've come to clear the air."

He shrugged. "So clear away." He patted the comforter, motioning for her to sit down beside him.

Her wiser self in charge for once, Leslie dropped into an overstuffed chair instead. "Tell me, Hugh, why did you really ask me to move in with you?"

"Haven't we covered that?" His expression showed impatience.

"Yes and no. You said something before about keeping the house because you thought I'd come back and live here. Was that what you were hoping for?"

"Was what?"

She hated it when he purposely evaded her questions. It meant he didn't want to pursue the subject. Hugh was prideful and stubborn. It'd be hard for him to accept separation and divorce—too much like failure. "I just wondered why you were procrastinating over the house. Was it not wanting to lose me? Or not wanting to admit defeat?"

"I've asked myself the same question. I'm not sure I know the answer."

"But if you don't know, who does?"

"Leslie, did you come to talk or to play Twenty Questions?"

"I give up," she said, totally frustrated. "Good-night, Hugh." So much for honest conversation. Hugh might desire her sexually, might mourn the loss of her as a wife, but that wasn't the same as wanting to start over. It was time for her to be savvier, more realistic. The smartest course was to keep her wits about her and not let Hugh rattle her. Otherwise he'd drive her crazy.

With that in mind, Leslie almost pulled out of the fishing trip the next afternoon. Why should she suffer the emotional turmoil of being in his presence? Because, she reminded herself, the payoff was a tidbit of retaliation. The old Leslie wasn't completely exorcised. She might as well give vent to one last impulsive act. Up till now she'd been too much of a doormat. Suffering Hugh's change of moods and raging ambivalence without fighting back. But she'd be darned if she'd participate in another one of those fakey love-bird situations with Hugh directing and starring in the role of the adoring husband. Today would be decidedly different. He still deserved a payback, doubly so after the way he'd treated her last night.

Despite a valiant attempt to hide it, the dismay on Hugh's face when she relayed Abby's invitation to tag along told Leslie mission accomplished. However, her distress was as great as his when they met Abby in the driveway and she gave them her news.

"What do you mean you aren't going?" Hugh looked as horrified as Leslie felt when Abby announced she wasn't well enough to go. Knowing a chaperon was on duty had made Leslie bold; she had planned to use the time together to give Hugh the impression she didn't give a darn about him. Now her safety net had been taken down.

"I'm just a bit under the weather," Abby assured them with a grandmotherly pat on Hugh's arm. "An allergy, I think. Probably the crepe myrtles or the honeysuckle. I'll be fine by tomorrow, once the antihistamines clear my head."

Despite her nervousness over being stuck out on a lake with Hugh, Leslie's fondness for the absurd was beginning to take hold. Abby's cheeks were rosy, her nose wasn't a bit red, and there hadn't been as much as a sneeze or sniffle. There was also a well-stocked picnic basket that showed Abby had spent a large part of the morning shopping and assembling. Their next-door neighbor was playing Cupid.

Hugh had to know something was afoot and he seemed even more uncomfortable at the notion of being alone with Leslie. "Then we'll wait until tomorrow so you can go along," he said to Abby.

"Oh, no, spoiling your day would make me miserable," Abby protested.

Hugh opened his mouth, then closed it.

Abby glanced Leslie's way and winked. This may be more fun than I planned, Leslie thought. Just seeing Hugh flummoxed like this was reward in itself. She winked back at Abby.

"Hugh's right," she added, joining the interchange. "Maybe we should wait till another time." Leslie hoped she sounded convincingly concerned. "The poor baby's been working so much all week, he deserves a break, not being stuck with me. If you're not there to teach me the fundamentals, he'll have to bait my hook and all that stuff. That would spoil his afternoon."

"Nonsense," Abby said. "You won't be any trouble to him at all. Besides, all those snacks I fixed will go to waste if you all don't eat them."

Hugh knew he was hooked—probably the only thing that would be all afternoon. His mind strained to sort out how this had come about. First, Leslie had stunned him by announcing she was coming along, then Abby had ratted out on him.

If he hadn't seen Les's expression when Abby gave them the news, he'd had sworn these two cooked it up together. *Women.* He hadn't realized they even knew one another. But Abby? Could she be up to something? Nah. Leslie, on the other hand…she had seemed determined to entrap him last night. Waiting for him in that skimpy little nightshirt. Delectable to look at, reminding him of what he had to forget. He shook his head. *Do not think of her or that nightshirt.*

"I know it's a 'teensy little' fish," Hugh explained, as he baited the line. "That's the whole idea. The big fish goes after the teensy fish and ends up caught." Hugh managed to sound exasperated, but he couldn't hide his grin. As expected, he wasn't getting much fishing done this afternoon, but surprisingly he *was* having fun. Leslie'd always had that effect on him.

That was one of the reasons he'd been drawn to her in the first place—her amazing ability to focus on the bright side of life. There hadn't been many bright spots in Hugh's life until he met her. After his father had deserted the family in Hugh's boyhood, there was no let-up from the constant drudgery of work. For him, as the only child, and for his mother. Sheer grit, and a nose constantly to the grindstone had allowed him to attend college, to make something of himself, the pattern of labor coming first becoming deeply ingrained.

Leslie didn't share his reverence for the work ethic. After her father's heart attack in his prime, she developed a philosophy that life was to be lived. Sure she did her job, and well, but she preferred to lend her energies to activities that were not subsidized by salary. To her, the real luxury of life was the enjoyment of it.

Hugh understood her reasons, but while Les had been deprived of a father figure, a modest trust fund had provided for her upbringing and education and, unlike him, she hadn't faced a childhood of near-destitution. He never wanted his children, their children, to be in that position. It wasn't just for himself he put in all those hours—it was for *them*.

But he'd missed Leslie's exuberance, their shared laughter…it had taken a total absence from her to make Hugh understand how much. He'd toiled almost as hard this past year at learning how to play as he had on the partner path at TGT. Today marked the first occasion, however, that he felt the full benefit of that learning experience.

He watched her throw a line into the water. Only a few minutes passed before the cork dipped. "A fish," she squealed, reeling and jerking so much that her catch—an empty Doritos package—came zipping into the air, smacking him right across the face.

"Not exactly," he said, peeling the paper off his face.

"Sorry," she said.

"Your bait's gone. Here…." He eased another minnow onto the hook.

For the next couple of hours, Leslie managed to feed every fish that approached her line, but failed to catch a single one. She was keeping Hugh so busy he hadn't managed to pull one in either.

"Oops, lost my bait again." She swung an empty hook in his direction.

"Careful. Those things are dangerous," he said, jerking out of harm's way, then gingerly reaching for her line to replace a minnow. "Sure you aren't letting these babies escape intentionally?"

Leslie giggled. It was a dandy day to be out on the lake, the pleasant breezes taking the edge off the summer heat. Too, Hugh's pontoon boat was surprisingly comfortable. She'd envisioned either a spartan rowboat with oars or maybe a motorboat, but not this monster-size craft that could easily accommodate eight. The deck was flat, better than berths if she and Hugh ever... She tried to erase the picture, but it wouldn't go away. Careful, she warned herself, you're losing your edge.

"Is the—" she leaned over and read the name printed on the side "—*Graceless* yours?"

"I bought it from Phil when he traded up to a cabin cruiser which Grace will deign to ride in occasionally. He bequeathed me the name and I couldn't bring myself to change it. Besides, *Leslieless* didn't have quite the same lilt."

Hugh's tone was bland, but Leslie still heard the implied rebuke. Was he forever going to needle her for leaving? He persisted in acting as though she'd snuck away in the middle of the night without his knowledge or consent. And she was getting tired of it. But no point in plowing that field again. If she hadn't managed to make Hugh see her side in the past, there was no reason to expect an epiphany now.

He'd cut the engine while they dined on Abby's provisions—hard Italian salami, crackers, fruit, olives, nut bread and flavored iced tea. Leslie leaned against the bench seat and stretched her legs in front of her. Hugh was at the wheel, an elbow propped across it, his hand holding a cluster of plump red grapes.

If it were dark, they could lie back to watch the stars, Hugh feeding her the grapes. The lapping waves would make the boat bob like a giant waterbed and.... Leslie drummed the vinyl seat in agitation. She needed to find another outlet to concentrate on—this one was going nowhere. Exacting any more revenge had lost its appeal, too.

"Tell me more about the practice," she said, bringing up one of the few safe topics.

"What else do you want to know?"

"Is it a general practice like TGT?"

"Pretty much. On a smaller scale of course. My cases run the gamut from traffic tickets to credit-card fraud, with a few wills, probates, and contracts thrown in."

"And businesses like Bert's textile company?"

"I have five or six on retainer. It helps with the rent and with Serena's salary."

"Oh, yes, *Serena*."

"What does that tone mean?"

"Just that whatever she's making, she's overpaid."

"Why do you say that? You've only talked to her on the phone a few times."

"Believe me, once is all it takes. Your secretary is rude and possessive. She makes a federal case of my every call. Like a wife doesn't have a right to speak to her husband."

"Like a wife?"

"You know what I mean." Leslie reached for an olive, embarrassed at forgetting herself. "Is she as objectionable to all your callers, or am I the exception?'' she asked. ''She didn't even know you were married, which seems a bit odd since all your other acquaintances had the impression I was simply off on a temporary assignment in France.''

''Serena doesn't know because I don't discuss my personal life with staff and if you don't stop yakking and start fishing, we're never going to get a bite.''

Leslie picked up her rod and reel, but continued chatting. ''Where did you find her anyway?''

''Quiet.'' Hugh hushed her with a finger against his lips.

She rolled her eyes. ''Am I disturbing you or the fish?''

''Both.''

For minutes, no one spoke. Hugh staring off in one direction, Leslie in the other. A tug on her line startled her. ''Hugh!'' she yelled, ''I think I've got one!'' She jumped to her feet.

''Settle down before you fall in the water.'' Hugh was behind her, his arms circling her and hands covering hers to help. ''Easy now, don't yank your rod around, just start reeling in slowly. My guess is you've snagged a big bass and he wants to fight.''

Together they landed the fish, Hugh holding up the squirming silver mass in admiration. ''This one's a real beauty. Close to five pounds.''

As Leslie watched the bass continue its frantic squirming, still trying to elude capture, she couldn't stand the pitiful struggle. ''Turn it loose,'' she cried, when Hugh started to drop the fish into the holding tank.

He looked at her askance. ''Are you crazy? After all that time and effort?''

''I don't care.'' Tears began forming in her eyes. ''Turn it loose. I feel so cruel.''

"Okay. It's your fish." A splash over the boat's side proved Hugh had done as instructed. "Thank you," she murmured with relief as she watched the creature swim rapidly away.

"You're welcome," he said, then laughed. "I'm just grateful you didn't have me hauling him to a veterinarian."

"I said thanks. Don't ruin your good-guy status with wisecracks."

"I'll try very hard not to." He looked at their empty fish chest with resignation. "Since we're not going to be reeling in our supper, how about a cruise around the lake instead?"

Leslie nodded happily, relieved Hugh wasn't berating her for being silly. For some reason, she hadn't equated "going fishing" with actually killing something.

As Hugh steered the pontoon, Leslie stole glances his way. Every now and then he would catch her eye and give her a smile, friendly yet wary, too. Okay, so her original "make Hugh miserable" mission was in shambles. But she was enjoying the day too much to care. And Hugh? *Is he enjoying this as much as I am?* she wondered.

It was dusk when they docked the boat at the marina. Hugh proclaimed himself hungry again and, at Leslie's suggestion, they stopped at a local catfish restaurant. The place was rustic, plate-glass windows plastered with posters announcing the Mesquite Rodeo and an upcoming country music concert, rough wood paneling lit with neon beer advertising. Red-plastic tablecloths covered the closely-set tables which were flanked by cane-bottomed chairs.

"Are you sure you want to eat here?" Hugh asked, taking a swallow from his bottle of beer.

"You had your heart set on fish and I spoiled it. The old man on the dock said they have the best cat-fish around."

"The fish here may have come from that same lake we threw the bass back in, you know. They may even be related."

"Really?" She eyed the platters being placed be-fore them. Fried catfish fillets, their cornmeal coating a golden brown, French-fried potatoes, cole slaw and hot yeasty bread.

"Nah, just kidding. These were purchased from a catfish farm or from a wholesaler. Maybe the corner grocery."

"That's better."

Hugh laughed. "That heart of yours hardens fast when you're hungry, doesn't it?"

"You bet."

"Little hypocrite," he growled.

"Hush and eat one of these." Leslie squirted a swiggle of ketchup on a mound of fries, then offered one to him. Hugh leaned across and took it in his mouth.

He chewed slowly, his eyes drinking her in, as-sessingly, approvingly. She wondered if a slice of po-tato could act as an aphrodisiac because she was experiencing sensations totally different from those that should have been conjured up from enjoying a meal. In fact, she could hardly taste the food anymore.

"So where do we go from here?" she asked, re-ferring to the evening.

"It's too soon to tell," he answered, deliberately misreading her question.

Silently, they continued eating and carefully studying one another, each aware that a line had been crossed.

CHAPTER EIGHT

LESLIE awoke to the irritating buzz of lawn equipment. *What idiot is disturbing the peace at dawn on a Saturday?* She glanced at the digital clock. *Gosh— ten o'clock.* The morning was half gone. Crawling out of bed, she made her way to the bathroom, passing by the window and catching a glimpse of the yard.

My idiot. Hugh, dressed in a faded red cropped shirt, cut-off jeans and a baseball cap, was busily mowing the front yard. As though sensing her observation, he looked up and waved. Waving back, and with a wide yawn, she headed off to the shower before the day was a total loss.

She felt drugged, sluggish. It wasn't in her nature to sleep so long and so late and she wondered if something could be wrong. She stared at herself in the bathroom mirror. No, she looked okay. Tousled, and with sheet imprints on her cheek, but okay.

The deep sleep was probably just another sign that her health was returning. There'd been so many restless nights over the past year. Last night was the first time since she'd returned to Dallas that she'd actually nodded off without any difficulty. *Could it be that I'm feeling happy today for a change?*

She slipped into bibbed shorts and T-shirt and went downstairs for a breakfast of cereal and coffee. The coffee helped. The grogginess was lifting and she felt ambitious enough to tackle a bit of yard work.

After applying sunblock and locating her tools and gloves in the small utility shed, Leslie headed toward the back garden. An hour passed as she lovingly turned the dirt in her vegetable plot and removed some surplus sproutings from the petunias and impatiens in the flower beds. A quick trip inside for more sunblock and a glass of water, then out again. Hugh had put away the lawn mower and edger and was now out back, too, measuring the pool chemicals. "Good morning, Sunshine," he called. "Glad to see you're finally among the living."

He seems happy, too. Happier than she'd seen him in a long time. Just as she'd been thinking that about herself. Leslie was about to comment on the situation, then reconsidered. Better to keep things casual for the moment. She looked around. "Where's the dog?"

"Pouting." Hugh laughed, pointing toward the pup lying under a chair, his paws covering his nose. "When I got out here, he was digging another trench under the fence. A little scolding and you'd think I'd beaten him."

"Poor Fritzie," Leslie cooed, reaching toward the dog. He inched her way, his tail wagging gratefully. "Daddy just wants you to be safe. If you get out of the yard, some mean old car might run over you."

"Daddy? Never have I referred to myself as 'Daddy' to that rascally cur. Keep that up and you'll have him spoiled rotten." Hugh smiled, the pleased expression on "Daddy's" face indicating he wasn't too worried with the notion.

"No office today?" She took a seat at the wrought-iron patio table.

Hugh came over and pulled out a chair for himself. "No, I decided to stay home and play catch-up. It's a good day, no pressing work. Do you have a problem with that?"

"Of course not. I was just curious." Hmm, Friday

afternoon and now Saturday. This was definitely unusual. Work really must be slow.

"Uh, have you checked on Abby?" she asked,
changing the subject.

"Abby's fine. I saw her all dolled up and taking
off to meet a friend for brunch. Bless her conniving
little heart—she just wanted us to be alone at the
lake."

So he saw through her guise. "If you knew what
she was up to, why didn't you simply refuse to go?"

"After all her trouble and that Oscar-caliber performance? 'I have an allergy,'" he imitated in a high-
pitched voice. "You'd have thought it was double
pneumonia."

Leslie laughed, feeling she owed their neighbor a
debt of gratitude. The outing had eased much of the
tension between her and Hugh, and for that she was
deeply appreciative.

"Why don't we make her really happy by going to
a movie and dinner?" he asked. "We could drive out
to the Galleria and wander around, then catch a five
o'clock feature and a burger afterward. What do you
say?"

"Great idea," she agreed, surprised at the invitation. A suspicious part of her had expected another
disappearing act. After all, it had been his way since
she'd returned home, even more so since their lovemaking. And since it *was* the weekend, Hugh could
well have had a date. Or perhaps not. After going
through the subterfuge with his new friends that their
being apart was due to Leslie's job opportunity over-
seas, and telling the Byerses they were working on
their relationship, maybe Hugh felt it wasn't politic
for him to be spotted with another woman. Then
again, all his girlfriends to date, except Serena, had

turned out to be false speculation. "When do you want to leave?" she asked.

"An hour? That should give us time to clean up and have a quick snack."

They drove to the Galleria, an upscale mall off LBJ Freeway, and browsed through the stores. Hugh purchased a pair of shoes at Nordstrom's and bought Leslie a scarf at Macy's, then they idly window-shopped and watched the skaters at the ice rink until the movie was due to start.

The film was a romantic comedy and although Hugh laughed in all the right places, Leslie noted that his attention wasn't completely on the screen. His arm was resting across the back of her seat, his hand occasionally brushing her shoulder.

Hamburgers at a nearby Chili's Restaurant followed the movie, then they drove home. "I shouldn't have drunk that last beer," Hugh said the minute they walked in the door. "All of a sudden I'm practically asleep on my feet. Would you mind if I said good-night and headed on upstairs?"

Leslie shook her head. She hadn't known how this day together would play out and now she had her answer. Hugh was being friendly, yet carefully avoiding intimacy. She flipped on the television, only intermittently listening to the late news while the events of the past two days competed for her attention.

Once the news was over, she clicked the remote, then switched off the lamps to go to bed. As she passed Hugh's room, the light shining under his closed door confirmed her thoughts that despite today's camaraderie, he was being cautious, determined to guard his privacy and keep an emotional distance.

*　　*　　*

When she awakened Sunday it was midmorning again. "This is getting to be a habit," she mumbled, rising to her feet. Must have been the yard work because she felt just as lethargic as yesterday. *Oh well, I'm still healing.*

Leslie was dressed and reading the newspaper when Hugh's car sounded in the garage. He entered, removing his suit jacket and hooking it over a doorknob. "Went to church," he said. "I would have asked you to come along, but you were sleeping so soundly, I decided to let you be. By the way, Abby called earlier and invited us to lunch—okay with you?"

"Sure," she agreed. For an estranged couple, they were certainly spending a lot of time in each other's company.

And the next week brought more of the same, companionable being the best description Leslie could find. Hugh was polite—more than that, warm and cordial. They talked of miscellaneous topics, and while the discussions were unvaryingly friendly, they were also…impersonal. It was as though both were walking on eggs.

He came home at six each evening, they ate early dinners at home or at restaurants, took Fritz for walks, chatted with people on the block. On Friday Hugh fished with Abby, Leslie declining the invitation to go along. Then a second Saturday when they worked in the yard and went out in the evening—this time to meet Grace and Phil Cotter at The Ballpark in Arlington for a Rangers baseball game.

Basically, it was what Leslie had asked for before she'd left. Almost. Yet there was a big void in their relationship, a missing intimacy. She remembered her earlier plan to treat Hugh as though he was a room-

mate. Without much effort on her part, that's exactly
the way it'd turned out. But the passion, the lifeblood
of their marriage was being deliberately curtailed.

"You did what?"

Hugh watched Leslie's brow furrow into a frown.
"I thought you'd be pleased," he said. "I let her go
this afternoon." He studied Leslie across the dinner
table as he stirred his iced tea. After her caustic remarks about Serena, Hugh had begun to think. He
hadn't been dissatisfied with his secretary's work performance per se, but Leslie's criticism had made him
reexamine a few incidents that he'd glossed over before.

Serena *was* possessive. Not just with Leslie, but
with any female who called the office. Even Grace
had commented on it. He'd been thinking about discussing Serena's attitude during her pending performance appraisal. She had forced the issue, however,
by her flirtatious shenanigans today. If he'd been the
employee instead of the boss, Hugh could have labeled the incident sexual harassment.

Never had he presumed the relationship with his
secretary to be anything but professional, but now, on
reflection, he could understand Serena reading more
into it.

She'd been part of the excitement of establishing
the new practice. The fact Leslie was gone and un-
accounted for made him look and feel disconnected,
unattached. He'd depended on Serena to fetch his dry
cleaning, make his haircut appointments, buy gifts—
the things a wife might take care of. No wonder she'd
seen herself as a helpmate. He'd erred by not sticking
strictly to business and there was no way to go back
and rectify his mistake.

In the end, he'd given Serena three months' severance pay and a glowing letter of recommendation. He'd miss her efficiency in the office, but it was better for both of them to make a fast, clean break.

"But why, Hugh? Is your practice in trouble?" Leslie's question cut through his thoughts and he paused in the act of salting his baked potato.

"Whatever gave you that idea?"

"I wondered if...you know...you've been around a lot more...and since the practice is new...maybe you needed to save on staff expenses." It was a logical assumption. It'd be nice to believe Hugh was spending evenings and Saturdays at home because of her, to believe that he'd really and truly changed, but she couldn't take that for granted.

It wasn't the first time she'd wondered whether he was all that busy. It could be that his firm didn't have enough clients to keep him occupied. Once the flow of business increased, however, Leslie suspected Hugh'd return to his workaholic ways and they'd go back to square one.

"If I was having money worries, wouldn't I have been more anxious to sell the house?" He set the salt shaker down and leaned on his folded arms.

"Well, possibly," she said.

"Why do so many of our conversations relate to finances?" Hugh asked. "Money is the least of my concerns right now. What's with you, Les? What does it take to please you these days? Freud himself couldn't figure you out."

"Thanks a lot! But look who's talking. All I did was inquire about the business. Was I supposed to assume you got rid of Serena simply because I complained about her?"

"Why not?" *Was it that hard for her to believe?*

He'd never seen Leslie so unsure, so questioning of all his motives. She took very little at face value.

"Even if you did," she continued, "what did you expect from me..." She paused a second. "A gold star?"

"No, dammit, but a little appreciation wouldn't have hurt." Hugh rose from the table and tossed his napkin down angrily. He realized it was childish to stomp off in a huff, but Leslie had done so many childish stunts, now it was his turn. He opened the French doors to the patio and stormed outside.

Leslie's words rolled around like marbles in Hugh's head as he grabbed a long-handled net and attacked the leaves in the pool with a fury. His mood didn't improve once he came back in. He needed to escape, to have somewhere private to come to grips with his feelings. The only private place he could think of was the office. Leslie'd probably complain about that, too.

Throughout the next morning and afternoon, Hugh's indignant response kept cropping up in Leslie's thoughts. She didn't mind admitting some insensitivity in the way she'd responded to his news about Serena. Undoubtedly, she should have been more tactful, rather than implying that Hugh let Serena go because business was bad. She should have thanked her lucky stars for the confirmation that Hugh and Serena were not involved, rejoiced in the fact the woman was gone and she didn't have to deal with her anymore. Her reaction should have been to leap up and click her heels together.

His crack about appreciation hit the bull's-eye, too. Even if his working too much had rankled her, she'd benefited from the results. Although embarrassed now to admit it, she'd never given him sufficient praise in that regard. No, she'd gone along blithely without uttering a word of thanks—never acknowledging all the material comforts his hard work provided. Another in her multitude of sins during their marriage.

When she received her first paycheck from Byers Textiles later that day, Bert suggested doubling her hours. "Business is improving," he'd said. "You must be my lucky charm." Leslie didn't know about lucky charms; the additional hours felt less like luck and more like pressure. She was nearing a decision point. If she wanted to move, she could soon afford an apartment. The problem was, she had no idea what she wanted anymore.

She stopped at a gourmet take-out market on the way home and picked up an assortment of salads for dinner. The temperature had zoomed past a hundred degrees today, much too hot for cooking.

Hugh was already there when she arrived at the house, dressed in swimming trunks and reclining in a lounge chair in the shade by the pool.

"Hello," she said.

"Hello," he responded, tone slightly cool, dark sunglasses covering his eyes.

She pitched her linen jacket across the back of a chair and sat near him. "There are deli salads in the refrigerator when you're ready."

"Fine," he said, still not putting himself out to make conversation.

"Bert's offered to double my hours."

This brought a reaction. "Oh?" He raised his glasses for a minute and studied her. "And did you accept?"

"Well, sure."

Pulling another chair up, she removed her pumps and propped up her stocking feet. They were swollen from the summer heat and it felt good to be off them. "I'm grateful for all you've done, but it only seems right, now that I'm pulling in a decent income, that I quit sponging off you and make some contribution to the utilities and phone bill."

To her amazement, he bolted from his chair, eyes blazing even through the tinted glasses. "Dammit, Leslie, you just won't quit, will you. I told you yesterday I wasn't hurting for money. What part didn't you understand?"

"I understood it all, but this is different."

"The heck it is. You're finally starting to get on your feet financially and you want to interrupt that progress by forking over your money like I'm some charity case."

Ironic he should be upset about the charity factor. That's what she had anguished about when he asked her to move in. "I seem to have hit a nerve."

"That's par for the course with you. You should come equipped with painkiller." He paced the deck, in a barefoot, but lawyerly fashion, composing his next words. "It's time to get this money hogwash cleared up once and for all. Truth be told," he continued as he perched on the edge of the lounger, "my practice is going better than I expected. But I know that bringing in the bucks carries no weight with you so I've soft-pedaled the earnings. That's okay, but don't insult me by suggesting I'm a failure." He got up. "I think I'll fix myself a drink." He went into the house.

Part of Leslie wanted to apologize, to tell him she was really proud that he'd risked going out on his own and was doing so well. Part of her wanted to explain that perhaps she'd never given him sufficient kudos for being successful because she'd simply taken it for granted that he would be. But a more rational part argued that nothing she could say would appease Hugh at the moment.

Later that evening, she was dozing in the lounger outside when Hugh approached. Apparently he was in a conciliatory mood as evidenced by the fact that he bore a bottle of wine, two stemmed glasses and a corkscrew.

Although swimming obviously wasn't his first priority, he was wearing swimming trunks—and doing them proud. Hugh's genetic makeup had bestowed on him a well-proportioned physique, but office demands had, in the past, prevented him from keeping in tip-top shape. Some apparent weight-machine workouts had more recently defined and toned his muscles so that he was amazingly sleek and fit now. It was difficult not to show or voice her approval.

Another difficulty was pretending not to notice the way he looked at her. Hugh opened the wine and set a glass on the table beside her, then took a seat himself at the foot of her chaise longue. "To making up," he toasted.

"Is that what we're doing?" Warily she picked up her glass and took a sip. The wine was a merlot, one of her favorites.

She'd hardly swallowed when Hugh, placing his glass on the concrete deck, pulled her feet into his lap. He began to massage them gently.

Leslie couldn't decide whether the massage was a case of old habits dying hard or an attempt at seduction. Foot rubs had always been sensual to her. No doubt Hugh remembered that. First the wine, now a foot rub. He was clearly putting the moves on her,

which didn't make a great deal of sense, considering
the barriers he'd erected when things got out of hand.

As he leaned over to kiss her, Leslie wondered if
he'd forgotten his earlier harsh words. She accepted
the kiss, savoring the familiar, yet exhilarating sensation of Hugh's lips on hers. But that was as far as
she intended to go.

Their disagreement this afternoon offered tangible
evidence that there were matters hanging, serious matters that should be discussed, resolved. She knew if
she gave in to her physical needs, any discussion
would be colored by those needs. Hugh might have a
talent for making love, then walking away, but Leslie
wasn't similarly blessed. It simply hurt too much and
she wasn't about to allow it to happen again. Before
they renewed the sexual side of their marriage, she
and Hugh had to make a commitment to the marriage
itself.

"Hugh, we've got to stop before this goes any farther," she told him as he bent his head for a second
kiss.

He straightened up and resumed his position at the
end of the lounger, feeling perplexed, hurt. He'd re-
thought their conversation about her increased hours
and concluded that he should have reacted differently.
But her pronouncement had set him on edge as he
waited for the other shoe to fall, the "now I can afford
to move" postscript. He'd been so prepared for that
earlier that he'd missed what he'd since decided were
her more telling words—those about contributing to
expenses, their *joint* expenses.

The wine was an attempt to make amends and
maybe provoke some straight talk about their future.
Instead it appeared he'd simply blundered again. "If

you say stop, we stop,'' he said, a chill to his voice. ''I'm not going to force anything you don't want.''

''It's not what I want or don't want. But we have problems to iron out before we get caught up in passion and it starts doing our thinking for us.''

He pursed his lips. ''I can't argue with that. So how do you propose we iron out those problems?'' He was stroking her feet again.

''Not this way.''

No, not this way. Events after their last night of ''amour'' should have etched that fact in stone. All common sense told him making love with Leslie right now would be a mistake. But common sense seemed to take flight when he was around her. At the moment, he didn't want to talk, he wanted to act...to hold her, to.... ''I'd sure like to change your mind.''

''And you probably could. So please...don't try to.''

''What's going to happen to us, Les?''

''I don't know,'' she answered honestly.

He stood. ''Well, while you're making up your mind just remember, we're bound to be lovers again, you and I.'' He waited a moment for the message to sink in, then added, ''In the meantime, the pool's handier than a cold shower.'' He performed a clean dive off the side and began to swim laps.

She watched him effortlessly execute the strokes in the water. *''Lovers,''* he'd said. *Not husband and wife.*

She knew she should be grateful for the increased office hours, but upon awakening Wednesday morning, Leslie resisted the thought of getting out of bed, in fact of moving at all. She grumbled at herself for agreeing to more work time, then commenced a silent condemnation of Bert for suggesting it and at Hugh for…well, at Hugh, on general principles and for the wine he'd plied her with last night.

She'd barely drunk a half glass, but felt like she had the mother of hangovers. Too bad Hugh'd already left. As it stood, there was no one besides Fritz to voice her complaints to.

"I need sympathy," she whined, "and all I get is a wagging tale. If I didn't know better, I'd swear you're entertained by my woes." When the dog responded by sitting up to beg, Leslie gave up, and stumbled on down the stairs miserably holding her stomach and muttering.

The queasiness continued into a second day, and then a third and Leslie began to worry. *Please. Not the hepatitis again.* Except for a need to catch up on sleep, she'd been doing great. She felt like crying. It wasn't fair after she'd come this far to have another relapse. Her only recourse was to schedule a doctor's appointment. She'd foolishly put off medical attention once and wasn't about to make that error again. Friday was her free day so she could go then.

Maybe all she needed were a few more vitamins to perk her up. Or maybe this was just a touch of summer flu. She couldn't take chances, however, and allow a second lengthy bout of illness to destroy her progress.

"You really should have contacted me the minute you got home," Dr. Poston scolded after Leslie supplied a history of the hepatitis and her subsequent medical traumas. "So I could continue to monitor you."

The doctor made several notes on her chart, then punched the intercom to summon the nurse. "Lucy will show you to a room and take your vital signs.

I'll be in afterward to check you over." She turned to her telephone as Leslie and the nurse left the room.

Half an hour later Leslie sat on the edge of the examining table, a sheet wrapped around her, feeling stunned. "But that's impossible!" she said, trying to deny Dr. Poston's diagnosis.

"You know how erratic my monthly cycle was before I started taking birth control pills. I'm sure I haven't missed a single pill. Besides that," she admitted grudgingly, "I've only had sex one time in the last year."

"Once is all it takes," Dr. Poston said.

"But are you positive of the diagnosis?"

The physician nodded indulgently.

"But how? Why?"

"How? I suspect the conventional way." The doctor smiled. Then she studied Leslie's face. "Is there a problem?"

Problem? How about problems? Her life was a mess at the moment. Living like a gypsy, married, but not married, unable to support herself. How could she fit a baby into this uncertain existence? And Hugh? Heaven only knew how he would react. Yes, one could say there were problems.

She searched for the right words to answer the doctor. "My husband and I are *estranged*." The word sounded foreign, unpalatable. "It's his baby," she hastened to add, "but this isn't something we would have planned at this particular time."

"I'm sorry. Then pregnancy must be a real jolt to you right now."

"I can guess what you're thinking, that I should be glad I'm not sick, that it's not the hepatitis." Leslie's voice trailed off. *I always dreamed of this moment, that it would be a joyful one, that I'd rush to Hugh, throw myself into his arms and announce…* Leslie felt as though her heart were being pressed in a vise. "Only…."

The doctor filled the void. "As to the why…you said you were taking antibiotics. Since you don't remember what kind and you've thrown away the bottle, there's no way to be certain they're the culprit, but some antibiotics do interfere in the effectiveness of birth control pills. If I were risking a guess, I say that's what happened here."

A tear trickled down Leslie's cheek and Dr. Poston handed her a tissue, then patted her shoulder comfortingly. "Maybe this will work out for the best. It often does."

"Maybe so. I'm just in a state of shock, that's all." *And not half as shocked as Hugh is going to be.* How in the world would she explain this to him? Would he think she'd deliberately gotten pregnant to hold him, or that it was just another example of her irresponsible ways?

CHAPTER NINE

LESLIE decided to take the coward's way out and not tell Hugh just yet. At least not until she'd seen the doctor again. She had several months before the pregnancy would start showing, more if Hugh viewed her weight gain as a return to her normal self.

Whatever her normal self was, that is. Leslie was beginning to decide there was no such thing as normal for her anymore.

She and Hugh had eased into a benign, mutually-tolerant living arrangement. With time and some careful nurturing, the arrangement could intensify. Therefore, she needed to avoid encumbering their relationship with new problems. She'd go to work, watch her pennies and let nature take its course. "In more ways than one," she groaned.

Of course she'd eventually have to share the news with Hugh, but perhaps when that day came, she would know better where he stood. Her position was no longer in doubt. Despite everything, she loved Hugh and couldn't bear the thought of living apart from him again. Knowing she was carrying his child only made those feelings stronger. But she refused to bind him to her unless that's what he also wanted. If he was over her, she wouldn't go along with resuming their marriage solely because Hugh felt obligated.

Thus, as though there were no change in the status quo, Leslie began a campaign of deception, a campaign which became tricky due to bouts of nausea plaguing her daily. "Generally a good sign," Dr.

Poston assured her. "There have been several studies linking morning sickness to healthy newborns."

"Mother Nature has a wicked sense of humor," Leslie answered. Fortunately, she wasn't one of those women whose so-called morning sickness lasted into the afternoon and evening. That would have made concealing her condition much more difficult.

"When's the due date?"

Bent over the sink in the ladies' lounge, Leslie was splashing cold water on her face when Pat Singer walked in and posed the question. Leslie looked up, startled.

Pat had hired on at Byers Textiles as a computer specialist right before Leslie left for France, so they didn't know one another well. Leslie was astonished that she'd been found out by a virtual stranger.

She winced. "I was hoping to keep the news to myself for a while. Is it that obvious?"

"Only to those who've been here. I have three, all boys," Pat explained. She then smiled consolingly. "With each pregnancy, I had to bolt from my desk so often those first few months, I felt like I was training to be a sprinter. Wretched, isn't it?"

"You can say that again." Leslie turned off the faucet and blotted her face with a paper towel.

"Does Bert know?"

Before Leslie could speak, Pat answered for her. "Silly question. If he knew, he'd be hanging a banner over the front door and calling himself Grandpa. It's no secret around here that he thinks of you as a daughter. Just wait till he finds out. He'll drive you crazy, pamper you to death."

Pat's goodwill was contagious and Leslie managed

a smile too. "You know him well. I'm glad he's away on a business trip right now."

"Tell you what. Let's go out to lunch and I'll give you a few tips on surviving pregnancy in the workplace."

Leslie pressed the back of her hand against her mouth. The mere mention of food made her stomach turn.

Pat gave her a little hug. "I know lunch sounds like the last thing you want, but you need the nutrition."

"Okay, but I don't promise to be scintillating company."

"Don't give it a thought. We'll take our lunch outside and park ourselves on a bench by the pond. If you don't feel like eating or talking, we'll feed the ducks instead."

Armed with Pat's noonday advice, Leslie stopped by the market on the way home and picked up a box of soda crackers and some fruit juices for work. Now that it was afternoon, she felt fine, even in the unyielding heat. It was as if she were two different people, the A.M. one sleepy and queasy and the P.M. one starved and full of energy.

From the bakery area, she selected a loaf of French bread, then bagged an assortment of salad mixings and added a sirloin steak to her basket. Heading down the frozen-food aisle toward the checkout stand, Leslie felt only a smidgen of self-reproach when a half-gallon of Blue Bell Dutch Chocolate ice cream caught her eye and instantly made its way to the grocery cart. *It's not as if you always eat this way*, she rationalized, recalling that lunch was only a fruit salad and yogurt.

When she got home, Hugh's car was already there. "Hi," he said, meeting her in the driveway, dressed in a pair of shabby cutoffs and a T-shirt.

"Nice legs," she remarked, glancing down.

"Why Mrs. Campbell," he quipped back, "I'm so pleased that you noticed." Hugh took the grocery bags from her arms and gave her a quick peck on the cheek. He peered inside the sack. "What's with all the juice and crackers? Looks as if you're opening up a preschool."

"They're for the office," she said, which was true.

"Don't you think people would prefer something fancier than plain old soda crackers?"

"Some of the staff are on diets," she hedged. Also true.

"Well, dieting is the least of your worries. You should be trying to gain weight, not lose any more."

The last thing Leslie wanted to get into was a discussion about her health. Hoping to avoid it, she placatingly said, "I got a steak for supper."

"That's more like it. I'll get the grill started."

Alone, Leslie emptied the sacks, the fibbing to Hugh taking a toll on her conscience. He was being so nice. Perhaps it was time to tell him about the baby. *No, not yet.* He might be more affable these days, but not once had he shown any desire for a reconciliation of their marriage. Until he did, she'd keep her pregnancy and her guilty feelings to herself.

An evolution began to take place, with each passing day bringing more closeness. But it was a just-pals closeness, one born of conversation and an exchange of ideas.

Hugh talked to her more candidly than he had at any time since their dating stage, but while those past discussions had been of ambitions and future plans, now he revealed tales of his childhood and opened up about the hurt and rejection he'd suffered when his father left. She suddenly had an inkling of what her leaving might have meant to him—not really the same, but too near a replay of past injuries to be easily forgiven. Leslie began to believe that only now was she really understanding the man she'd married.

Likewise Hugh listened to her stories, some of them happy recollections of vacations and special holidays, others sad remembrances from the tragic period after her father's heart disease inexorably altered the family's existence.

Leslie told Hugh about the long days spent waiting outside the hospital's coronary care unit and about her inability to suppress a shiver whenever an ambulance siren blasted the air. How different their lives might be, Leslie thought, if these exchanges with Hugh had taken place years ago.

After that night at the poolside when she'd rebuffed his overtures, Hugh hadn't initiated lovemaking again, but his behavior was changing course, not in the manner of a racing current, but slowly, like a meandering stream. And the changes were positive. Simple things like stopping by the video store on the way home for a movie to watch together. Plucking radishes from the garden and presenting them to her in the fashion of a bouquet as she was making a salad. Then the next day, bringing her the real thing. Leslie couldn't remember how long it had been since he'd brought flowers outside the confines of a formal occasion.

"I know the yard's in bloom now, but these made me think of you." It was a bunch of gerber daisies in a variety of colors, the kind Leslie had often bought herself to place on the coffee table.

"Thank you," she said, searching for a vase from the cabinet over the ovens. Hugh's gesture wasn't expensive, but it enriched her as much as a million dollar bequest. It also made her want his love and devotion more than ever.

He came over and reached around her, retrieving a vase from the farthest corner. "Is this the one you're looking for?"

They'd purchased it from a potter at one of the First Monday Trade Days in Canton, a small town east of Dallas. During trade days, the area boasted acres of booths and shops and served as an outlet for an eclectic mix of artisans and craftspeople.

Leslie had been sentimental about the vase. It was one of their few purchases during those lean years in college and right after, when necessities gobbled up all their money. She valued the piece more than any of the pricier accessories they'd added once their lifestyle became more affluent.

"Yes, that's the one." She twisted around to smile at him. Still holding the vase, Hugh propped his other hand against the cabinet door and bent his head to kiss her. It was the longest, slowest, gentlest kiss Leslie had ever received, at first only their lips touching, as though Hugh was being cautious not to allow any other part of their bodies to come in contact. Then he folded her into his arms.

"Let's go out for dinner," he whispered, once a necessity for air had forced them to end the kiss.

Breathing heavily, Leslie nodded. If they were going to have a meal tonight, someone else would have to prepare it. That kiss from Hugh had left her weak in the knees. She was liable to set the kitchen on fire if she tried cooking right now. Eating out was much safer.

Hugh's breathing was as heavy as Leslie's. *I'm becoming a master at evasive tactics*, he thought as he headed upstairs to get rid of his tie and exchange his dress shirt for a polo, putting some momentary distance between them.

He had to remember that Leslie had erected a stop sign as far as sex was concerned. He'd chanced that kiss and she'd participated, but he doubted she'd go any farther and he didn't want to be rebuffed again. Getting out was the best way to accomplish that.

Despite her no-sex dictum, it seemed as if he and Leslie were growing closer. He'd been trying to nurture their relationship, and at times he felt optimistic. At least she hadn't jumped up and moved out when Bert increased her office hours. *But she still could.* He couldn't eliminate that fear from his mind. Hugh felt like he was holding a time bomb ticking off an unknown number of minutes before it exploded. If only a miracle would materialize before the bomb's clock ran down and his life was shattered again. Sometimes *miracles* do happen.

"So when will you tell him about the baby?" A week had passed since that unsettling kiss and Leslie was eating lunch with Pat Singer, a daily occurrence now.

Having a friend like Pat was a godsend. Not only was she a veteran of three pregnancies and brimming with helpful advice, but she also possessed an empathy that Leslie had been unable to tap in anyone else.

"I know I need to tell him soon, but things are going so well," Leslie said.

"Lucky you're slim as a reed. That buys you a bit of leeway. How's the nausea?"

"It doesn't last as long, but it's still touch and go

when I first get up. Fortunately Hugh's usually at work by then.''

"Has he hired another secretary?''

"Yes, and she's great. I never met Serena so I can't compare, but it's hard to believe she could be any more attractive than Natalie.''

"And you're not jealous of her?''

"No. I don't think she's interested in anyone else's husband. It's more than that, though. Hugh's not the type to play around. I realize that now. He's too honorable.''

"You trust him," Pat stated.

"Yeah." Leslie grinned. "With my life, my heart," she rubbed her midsection, "our baby.''

"Then you'd better tell him about the little guy, don't you think?''

Leslie nodded. "Not quite yet though. Don't ask me what it is, but I'm waiting on something." Leslie couldn't admit that she was still holding out hope that before she did, Hugh would first declare his love, would ask her to be his wife—in every meaning of the word—again.

"Well, don't wait too much longer," Pat said. "He's probably going to be a tad hurt as it is. And angry, too, especially if he discovers the news on his own.''

"I'll tell him soon.''

Hugh's pattern of Friday afternoons with Abby continued. The activity was good for their neighbor, and for Hugh also. The fishing duo continued to invite Leslie along, and she continued to graciously refuse. She wasn't being a martyr—it was self-preservation.

Being on a boat was not a good idea for a pregnant woman where the rocking might revive a bout of nausea. Besides, Leslie's one foray at the lake had convinced her she was no angler. So she let the two have their fun alone. She used the Friday afternoons to lounge around the house and prepare to cook "the catch of the day," cleaned and filleted, of course.

On a Friday morning in late September, Leslie raced for the bathroom the second she heard Hugh leave. Yesterday her stomach had been calm and she'd dared to believe the siege of morning sickness might be over. After all, she was nearing the end of the first trimester.

Was she ever wrong. Relieved that today wasn't a workday, Leslie was slumped on the floor, leaning her head against the cool porcelain of the tub when she opened her eyes and saw a man's tasseled loafers. Her eyes moved upward—suit pants, jacket, tie...furious expression. "I thought you'd gone," she said.

"I forgot my wallet and came back. Good thing, too," he said angrily. He took a washcloth from the towel rack and ran it under the faucet to dampen before giving it to Leslie. "When did this start?"

"A couple of months ago." *Darn.* This wasn't the way it was supposed to be when she told Hugh about the baby. She'd planned a cozy scene out by the pool, the two of them having a nightcap—his champagne, hers apple juice. She would wait until dark, when the moon and stars were out, a romantic setting, she wearing something flowing and sexy.

Revealing all while doubled up on the bathroom floor in a wrinkled cotton nightshirt, her teeth unbrushed and hair a mass of tangles was certainly not even close to her scenario.

Expression and tone softening, Hugh said, "I feel like a cad for not noticing." How in hell could he have been so blind to Leslie's suffering, especially

considering how difficult it was to keep his eyes off
her whenever they were together? "If this has been
lasting for a while, your weight's probably plummet-
ing again." It took all of his strength to keep the panic
from his voice. Removing his jacket and rolling up
his shirt sleeves, he declared, "You're going to the
doctor today."

When she opened her mouth to protest, he interrupted, "No arguments. I insist." He sat on the edge
of the tub and turned on the water, twisting the knobs
to adjust the temperature and testing it with his inner
wrist.

"I've seen a doctor," Leslie admitted, over the roar
of the bath water.

"What did he say? Has the hepatitis flared up
again? Are you overdoing it? You don't have to work
so much, you know. Unless you're so damn anxious
to be on your own and away from me." Hugh felt the
terror so strongly, he couldn't control his words.
Concern for Leslie mixed with white-hot anger that
she hadn't shared her problems. He turned off the water, then stood up and grabbed the hem of her nightshirt, ready to rip it over her head.

Leslie pulled it from his fingers. "I'm perfectly
healthy."

"I can tell," he snarled. He and Leslie had had
many a skirmish, but until her illness, she'd never lied
to him. He had to have the truth now. "I want some
straight answers, Les."

"As I said, I'm perfectly healthy." She paused before adding, "For a pregnant woman."

Leslie had never fully appreciated the adage about
being able to hear a pin drop, but that was an apt
description for the silence following her announce-
ment.

Hugh's stunned reaction and the unconcealed distress on his face wounded Leslie to the core. What had she expected—that he'd madly embrace her and shout hosannas while declaring it wonderful news? As the hurt deepened, Leslie knew that's exactly what she'd hoped for.

Hugh dropped down onto the edge of the tub. "I had…I assumed…it never occurred to me. Oh, man…." His voice trailed off. *A baby.* The possibilities were overwhelming…he, Leslie, a child. Maybe this was the miracle he'd been hoping for. He wanted to pull her into his arms, tell her he was thrilled with the news, to cover her face with kisses. But how did Leslie feel? His brow furrowed and his lips pursed in a frown. She didn't look any too happy at the moment. "When? How far along are you?"

"Figure it out for yourself," she snapped. "Or are you insinuating the child may be someone else's?"

Hugh let loose with an expletive.

"I'm almost three months along—okay?" Leslie said. "And don't look so stricken. The baby and I won't interfere with your life, if that's what you're upset about."

If shaking her had been an option, Hugh would have taken it. "What I'm upset about is your not telling me and letting me find out accidentally. First the illness and now the pregnancy."

"I was going to tell you."

"So what were you waiting for?"

She had no answer. She couldn't confess that she was waiting for him to love her. She had too much pride for that.

"Well?" he prodded.

"I was afraid—afraid you'd be as mad as you are."

"I'm not mad."

"Oh, right. Your complexion is always that shade of red your eyes bulge all the time."

Hugh studied himself in the vanity mirror. "My eyes are not bulging and my face is merely sunburned from playing golf yesterday." Hugh was beginning to see things from a different viewpoint. Was Leslie thinking he wouldn't want the baby? Foolish woman! That ticking bomb had finally quietened. It appeared he was going to have the luxury of more time to convince her they belonged together after all. His image changed from a scowl to an impish grin.

Leslie wondered just what that grin of Hugh's meant, but she wouldn't give him the satisfaction of asking. "You're impossible," she charged.

"Maybe a little," he agreed softly, turning and extending a hand to touch her face. "Take your bath and I'll fix you breakfast. Are you up to eating something now?"

"No, not yet." She was feeling none too kindly toward him despite the softening of his attitude and the conciliatory caress. "You go on to work. I'll be fine."

"I'm not going anywhere," he answered stubbornly, mouth set, firmness restored. "We have too much to talk about."

Hugh propped his hands on the kitchen sink and stared out into the yard. Early in their marriage, he and Leslie'd talked about children, how many they would have, what names they liked...but it had been something for the future, tossed about the way young couples were wont to do. This wasn't the future, this was now—almost. And Hugh was ecstatic.

He called his office to say he wouldn't be in, then phoned Abby to beg off from their scheduled fishing excursion. "Only one more call," Hugh told Fritz, who was tap dancing about his feet waiting to be fed as his master dialed that last number.

Breakfast was on the table and Hugh reentering the back door when Leslie came down. "Toast and cantaloupe," he announced, helping her with her chair, then sitting down across from her. "I was afraid any real cooking smells might bother you."

"Very considerate," she said, forcing a bite of the toast and chewing methodically.

Hugh saw that she was not at all interested in eating, but was preoccupied with composing a statement, probably one destined to irritate him. What she said didn't matter anyway, because he'd already prepared his own speech, outlining actions he was bound and determined Leslie would accept.

"Hugh," she began, "as I was trying to tell you upstairs, this doesn't change anything between us. We might as well get that straight right now." She was still resolute that her pregnancy not be the sole impetus for a reconciliation.

He put down his coffee mug. "Wrong. It changes everything. You may have every intention of running off again, but let me make it perfectly clear that during this pregnancy you're not going anywhere without me. If I have to slap handcuffs on us to keep you by my side, then so be it."

He pointed a finger at her. "There will be no running off with my child. Understood?" He rose and started pacing, unable to keep still. "Oh, and you can also forget about selling the house right now." Hugh had stopped the pacing and was leaning against the sink, one hand gripping the stainless steel rim to immobilize himself. "I've already yanked that sign out of the yard and notified the realtor."

"And I have no say-so in any of this?"

"Not a word, Leslie. Not a single word." He relaxed his grip on the sink and stuffed his hands in his pockets. "Finish your breakfast. I've canceled all my commitments today so—"

"No way," she protested. "I won't have you hovering over me and playing guard dog for the next six months. And I won't allow you to make unilateral decisions about my future."

Hugh paused a second, realizing he had gone a tad too far. "Okay," he said. "Tell you what...I'll swear not to be a 'guard dog' if you'll make me a promise in return."

"What kind of promise?"

"Not to leave. To live here and put off all talk of separating again until the baby is at least six months old."

"That's a year from now."

"Will you give me the year, Les?"

Ultimately, she had agreed, primarily because she wanted to, but rationalizing that it was a practical decision. Hugh had momentarily backed down, but she could tell he was a man possessed. He wouldn't give her a moment's peace until she conceded, and if she tried to move into an apartment, he'd likely make good on his threat. Not going as far as the handcuffing, but putting every other imaginable obstacle in her path.

Leslie wasn't about to risk the turmoil. It wouldn't be good for her or for the baby. And whatever it took to protect her child, she would do. She felt a love for this unborn infant that she wouldn't have believed possible. If everything had been solid between her and Hugh, then she would be supremely happy. But it was all too obvious that Hugh—good, old dependable

Hugh—was doing the correct thing. He hadn't asked for "forever afters," just for a measly year, long enough to see her through the birth of the baby and for her to get back in the swing. But perhaps it was a step in the right direction.

"Oh, he couldn't be more wonderful," she told Pat over lunch a month later. "Home at night, solicitous, bringing me little gifts, waiting on me. But I can't help feeling it's only because of my condition. Having him on those terms just isn't what I want."

Pat's suggestions that Leslie might be looking a gift horse in the mouth didn't ease Leslie's mind. Nor did Hugh's cheerful sharing of their news with his mother at her retirement village in the Ozarks and with all their friends.

The first to hear was Phil Cotter whom Hugh called to check on Leslie's doctor, a fellow obstetrician. "She's in good hands, pal," Phil had told him. "We did our OB residency together. I was impressed then and still am." Thus reassured, Hugh set out to alert the world.

"You'd think you're the only expectant father in history," Grace teased over dinner at The Mansion, one of Dallas's most exclusive restaurants. Hugh had asked the Cotters to join them for a celebratory meal.

"There have been others?" Hugh asked, eyebrows raised, causing Grace to shake her head in amusement.

"I suppose I should issue an advance warning that I plan to bore everyone with a walletful of baby pictures, too," Hugh continued, more ebullient than Leslie could ever remember. He reached over and took her hand, bringing it to his lips for a quick kiss. "I didn't think I'd ever be this happy."

It was as if the words were for her alone and Leslie

could hear the unspoken "again." Still, her fears that Hugh's attentions had less to do with her and more to do with the coming event were not entirely eased.

Nor did the dinner a week later at Bert and Molly's. Hugh had been trying to get Leslie to cut her work-week back to two days, but she had adamantly refused. She simply would not relinquish all control over her life. As long as the doctor gave her the green light, she would decide by herself how many work-days she was capable of handling. She was aggravated that Hugh took advantage of the social opportunity to appeal to Bert.

"I think she's overdoing it, don't you, Bert? From what I read, a number of first pregnancies end in miscarriage. I don't want to take any chances."

"Poor Bert." Leslie gave a strained laugh, trying not to let her irritation show. "Trapped in the middle of a domestic squabble." She turned toward Hugh. "*I* don't want to take any chances, either. The doctor assures me it's good to remain active. If I get tired, I come home early. Fortunately—" she winked at Bert "—I have a compassionate boss."

Bert, however, looked concerned. "Maybe Hugh's right," he said.

Molly patted Hugh on the arm, her warm hazel eyes staring into his with amusement. "Why is it the strongest of men become nervous wrecks over motherhood? Leslie's glowing, can't you see? And as for you, Bert, Leslie's going to be just fine. This time next year, we'll baby-sit and those two can run off and make another baby."

It was a well-meant sentiment, but the thought caused a clutch in Leslie's throat. Who knew what next year would bring? She glanced Hugh's way. His

neck was flushed. *He's embarrassed.* She couldn't recall ever seeing Hugh look so edgy.

"Molly's comments seemed to disturb you," Leslie
began on the drive home. She needed to have more
insight into Hugh's plans for their future, but every
time she tried to bring it up, he had put her off.

His response tonight was no more revealing, as he
tapped the gearshift deep in thought. *Hell yes, I was
disturbed. Bert and Molly are talking about baby-
sitting and I have no idea whether you'll even still be
here.* Hugh had tried to quiet his fears by assuring
himself Leslie had promised to stay around for a year,
but he couldn't help worrying about what would happen then. He wanted a commitment for all the years
to come, not just one. But he was afraid to push for
too much, terrified she'd refuse. Instead of answering,
he reversed the question on her. "What about you,
Les? How would you feel about another child?"

"Under the circumstances, I'm sure you'd say I
was doubly irresponsible if that happened."

He pulled over to the curb and shifted into Park,
but didn't kill the motor. Resting an arm across the
steering wheel, he turned her way. "What's the message here, Les? That I'm faulting you for this pregnancy. If so, it's an unfair accusation and you damn
well know it."

"That's not what I meant. I just wondered...our
future is so...so uncertain," she stammered.

"I know, but let's give ourselves a chance and see
what happens," Hugh said, his tone deliberately calm.
Leslie apparently wanted a cutoff date for their marriage. What was she planning to do—trot around the
world with the baby in a backpack? That wasn't going
to happen. He was determined to persuade her they

had a marriage worth keeping, that he'd never let her go again. Never.

Since Leslie's return to Dallas, summer had simmered into fall, then fall faded into winter. Holidays came and went. She and Hugh'd hosted a Halloween party as reciprocation for some of their many invitations, had been guests of Bert and Molly and the rest of their family for Thanksgiving, then decorated the house together for Christmas.

Hugh's mother flew in from Arkansas for Christmas, and after opening presents and talking to Leslie's mom by telephone in the morning, the three of them had gone to share Christmas dinner with Pat and her husband Tommy. The passing of the old year and greeting of the new one was spent with Grace and Phil.

Hugh's practice was becoming busier by the day. He'd begun a routine of arriving home at six or six-thirty to have supper with her and had added an associate to the practice to help take up the slack. But he was burning the candle at both ends. Frequently, from her lonely bed in the guest room, Leslie heard him climbing the stairs long after midnight and she knew he'd been catching up on work brought home from the office.

She told herself she should be happy he was making such an effort at domesticity and reminded herself that she'd finally gotten what she'd been asking Hugh for all those years. Attention and a social life. But the motivation was all wrong, the results insufficient.

In a heated moment, she told him so. "You don't have to do this," she said when he handed her a bouquet of violets in mid-January.

"You're very welcome," he responded sarcastically.

"I'm tired of all the pretense. You're only doing it because you feel guilty that I'm big as an elephant and I...I...." She started sobbing and Hugh wrapped her in his arms.

"I don't feel an ounce of guilt and you...don't you realize how beautiful you are?" he said, patting her protruding stomach and holding her until the sobs subsided. "There's no pretense, Les. I want you and I want our child." He kissed her on the forehead.

His tenderness was welcome, and his declaration comforting. He was offering her sympathy, affection, devotion. But he hadn't even broached the possibility that she share his life permanently. Nor had he attempted any more lovemaking.

CHAPTER TEN

HUGH unbuckled his seat belt and retrieved his briefcase from beneath the seat in front of him. As he stood and waited for the cabin door to open, he felt the nervousness heighten and knots begin to form at the base of his neck.

Keeping his wits about him during the flights to Houston and the trial preliminaries was easy. It was on the trip back to Dallas that the tension began to take hold. Until he got home and found Leslie there, insecurity dogged him like his own shadow. He wondered if it would always be like that.

She'd never said she intended to stay. *He'd* been the one who'd dictated an extra year of living together. She hadn't argued, had seemed to go along with him, but he'd given her no choice. Had she simply acquiesced for the moment, biding her time?

Hugh knew he was being ridiculous. Where was a woman almost eight months pregnant going to go anyway? *Face it, Campbell*, he told himself. *Whether she wants to be or not, Leslie's stuck with you. For the time being anyway.*

The slam of a car door signaled Hugh's homecoming. Leslie hated the way her heart sped up whenever she heard him arrive. It reminded her too much of their old life—she waiting idly for hours, leaping to her feet whenever a car approached, only to be disappointed when it wasn't Hugh. There was no way she'd allow herself to regress to that sorry state.

170

And you're on the verge of it, you know, she admonished, ruefully acknowledging that it took every ounce of willpower to keep from running—or waddling, considering her advanced condition—outside to greet him. Instead, bedraped in her extra-large terrycloth robe, she stayed put in the easy chair, swollen feet and legs propped on an ottoman.

The doctor had warned her not to ignore the swelling—as if she could—and advised her to keep off her feet as much as possible. She was heeding the advice, but not happily. Lately she'd gone few places, except to work, and Hugh had engaged a cleaning service for the house. Her flower and vegetable gardens provided no outlet since Dr. Poston recommended against gardening. For an active type, Leslie was enduring a span of indolence that would do a couch potato proud.

She heard Hugh enter the back door and advance through the house to join her in the cozy den. He set his briefcase on a table and came over to kiss her forehead. "Miss me?" he said, and Leslie detected a wariness in his tone, as though he might be afraid of the answer.

She checked her watch. "You've been gone exactly two days, twelve hours and fourteen minutes, give or take a minute or two."

"Nice to know you're keeping track." He plopped down on the sofa and untied his shoes. "I'm beat."

Leslie scrutinized his face. The lines around his eyes were more pronounced and a trace of five o'clock shadow darkened his jaw. He did look exhausted. "You shouldn't do this to yourself," she said.

"Do what?"

"Keep up this frenetic pace. You fly back and forth between here and Houston two or three times every week. Anyone would think you own shares of Southwest Airlines.''

"Actually, I do," he said.

"Well I doubt the stock would tumble precipitously if you took fewer flights.''

"Are you suggesting I'm gone too much? Dammit, Les, I'm doing the best I can. I can't be in Dallas every minute. I'm not going down there for the sights, you know. This is important.''

"Our baby's important, too."

"I know that, but it's not due for weeks. This case is going on now.''

"I don't care about the case. Besides, I have a hunch the baby's going to come early.''

"Did the doctor say so?"

"No. But…oh, just call it a gut feeling, pardon the pun.''

He smiled. "Gut feeling aside, I think I'll go with the professional opinion. Besides, if your intuition's on target, why haven't you left your job yet?''

"My job's in Dallas, not two hundred miles away.''

"But you're the one with the hunch. I'd prefer that you start the maternity leave, just to be on the safe side. Tell you what—you give notice and I'll see what I can do about the jaunts to Houston.''

"I stop working and you 'see what you can do'? Now, why am I suspicious of the way you phrased that? Sounds like I'd be guaranteed to draw the bad end of that bargain. I go on leave and you keep up your marathon flight schedule anyway.''

"Do we have to hash this out tonight?'' Wearily, Hugh ran his hand down his face. "A week or so longer and I promise I'll be through with the trial. We'll still have ample time to get ready for the baby.''

"Unless it's early. I was. Two weeks as a matter of fact."

"So? According to my mother, I was born three weeks past the due date. You're worrying unnecessarily."

"Says who? Mr. Hugh Campbell, world renown authority on pregnancy and childbirth?"

"Ouch." He gave an exaggerated wince.

"It's happening again." Leslie's voice was solemn.

"What's happening?"

"You. Working too much. And when I express my concerns, you trying to beg off from a discussion. Just like before. You've got an associate now, Hugh. Let him make these trips to Houston. You don't have to handle every detail."

"You know better than that, Les. This is a big case and the client is paying *me* to handle it, not some fuzzy-cheeked associate."

"You always have an answer." She sighed. "We've come full circle. You working day and night. Me complaining. The 'big case' in Houston. Déjà vu."

"Does that mean you'll take off again, too? Timbuktu maybe?"

Incredulously she looked at him and then down at her stomach. "Right. Almost eight months pregnant and I'm going to travel to the ends of the earth. If you're worried, you could carry out your ridiculous macho threat to handcuff us together."

"Maybe I should at that." Hugh left the room, returning momentarily with a bottle of beer. He took a generous swig, then looked at her with eyebrows raised as if poised for her comeback.

"Let's just call a truce for tonight and forget the sniping," she relented. "We do too much of it."

Hugh crossed to her chair and stroked her hair. "I agree. Honey, I know I need to be home more and I'm doing everything in my power to achieve that goal."

Leslie had heard it all before. Reasonable or not, she didn't want to listen to his excuses anymore. But Hugh *was* tired and he deserved a little sympathy. "We don't need to get into this tonight. You're bushed and I'm not feeling too perky myself. There's sandwich stuff in the refrigerator for your dinner. If you don't mind, I'm going on to bed." With a great deal of effort she rose to her feet.

Hugh wished she'd stay with him, but knew that was being unfair. It was getting late and Leslie needed her rest. "No, go ahead. I'm so relieved I don't need to rush out for those handcuffs that I'll even come tuck you in."

As intended, the teasing provoked a smile from Leslie. Even with the tension that existed between them, it was getting easier to draw those smiles. He'd plotted a campaign for handling Leslie. Lots of to-getherness, no smothering, no being overbearing, no bickering back and forth. He'd been pretty successful, except for the bickering part. He wanted to keep it light between them, to make her laugh, to show her he'd learned how to smell the roses too. He wanted to win back her love.

He'd just have to try harder, Hugh thought, as he went to the refrigerator and assembled a ham sand-wich. He chewed it as his thoughts chewed on him.

He wanted desperately to touch her, to hold her. Restraining himself was an effort worthy of a saint. He was no saint, but he had to keep his hands to himself until he had a better understanding of Leslie's feelings about him. *Regardless of all my efforts, what if she leaves anyway?* The notion made Hugh want to punch his fist through a wall. Well, if she did leave, there was no place on earth she'd be able to hide from him. Wherever she went, this time he'd be on her trail like a bionic bloodhound.

Angrily, Leslie plucked the handwritten note off the refrigerator door, causing the ceramic magnet to drop to the tile floor and shatter. "Despite all my protestations, he's gone again," she said to Fritz, crushing the notepaper into a ball and tossing it across the room.

"But I'll be back tomorrow," Hugh announced, placing his briefcase on the kitchen table.

"You scared me half to death," she said, backing against the cabinet, hand across her thumping chest. "I thought you'd already gone."

"I was about to. I wrote the note because I didn't want to wake you, but I couldn't leave without saying goodbye." He placed two fingertips against the pulse of her neck and felt the rapid beat. "I didn't mean to scare you." His lips replaced the fingertips, the kiss slowly exploring the plane of her cheek before finally settling on her lips. Leslie couldn't resist. Her arms curled around his neck.

The kiss was still pulling at her senses hours later, but Leslie was doing her best to ignore that pull. "Right before my eyes he's falling back into old patterns," she said to Pat over coffee at a shop across the street from their office. "Work will always be more important to him when push comes to shove. He'll never have his priorities straight."

"The Hugh I've met and been hearing about for the past six months bears no resemblance to a guy who doesn't have his priorities straight," Pat attempted to soothe her. "He seems as excited as you about the baby."

"Oh, he is in his own way. But his heart still belongs to the law. He'll probably be in some courtroom instead of with me in the delivery room when the baby's born."

Leslie traced her index finger around the rim of the coffee cup. "I can picture myself driving to the hospital while he's off consoling a client...." She took a sip of coffee, realizing she was becoming overwrought, but seemingly unable to calm herself. "I need Hugh at my side—not halfway across Texas."

"Have you told him how you feel?"

"I've tried—he doesn't seem to understand."

"Then you'll have to make your feelings clearer."

Sitting at her desk later that morning, Leslie was contemplating Pat's advice that she level with Hugh and tell him honestly and straightforwardly how much she needed him right now. If she put it to him like that, would it do any good? Or would Hugh think she was acting like a spoiled brat determined to have her own way?

"You look like Sad Sack on a bad day."

"Who?" she asked, glancing up to see Bert Byers standing over her.

"Sad Sack. An old cartoon character." He propped a hip on the corner of Leslie's desk.

"I suppose I'm a little tired."

"Then go home early and start taking it easy. It's time for me to pull rank. I don't want to see you around here until I'm a grandpa."

"That's a wonderful idea," Leslie agreed. She'd thought over Hugh's words last night and realized he was making sense about her giving up work. Now the decision had been taken out of her hands. "Thanks,

Bert." She planted a kiss on his shocked face and began gathering her belongings.

Immediately upon arriving home, she dialed Hugh's office. Since he'd made an issue of it last night, she wanted to tell him she'd begun her maternity leave. His secretary would track him down so she could share the news.

"I'm sorry, Mrs. Campbell," Natalie told her an hour later. "I've checked everywhere but I can't locate him."

"Are you certain?" Impatience gnawed at Leslie. She'd never attempted to contact Hugh before when he made trips out of town. His frequent calls made that unnecessary. But his usual calling time was hours away. Oh well, she'd just have to be patient until he phoned. Then they'd talk calmly and rationally.

She lay down on the couch to wait. An hour passed without a single ring—not that she'd expected it so soon. However, Leslie, growing more restless with every second, found herself with another agenda. Suddenly, she was gripped by an intense spasm in her abdomen. Fifteen minutes later another one came.

She wondered if her premonition had turned into reality. Surely not this early! Over four weeks remained before her due date. Panicked, she called the doctor, then summoned Abby from next door. After leaving a message with Hugh's secretary, they headed for the hospital post-haste.

It was happening just as she'd feared it would. True, she wasn't driving herself—Abby was at the wheel—but when she delivered, she'd be alone. The pains were accelerating so rapidly, Hugh'd never make it back to Dallas by then, even if he could be found.

*   *   *

"Mr. Campbell, I'm Mary Poston." Doctor Poston intercepted Hugh as he tore down the hospital corridor toward Leslie's room an hour later.

"Is...is my wife okay?" Hugh asked breathlessly.

"She's fine. In fact, you got here just in time to drive her home. The pains stopped shortly after she checked in. False alarm."

Hugh heaved a sigh of relief. An uneasiness had brought him home a day early. When he'd driven into the garage, Leslie's car was parked in its space and the house showed signs that she'd been home after work. He called Abby thinking she might be there, but there was no answer at Abby's. He then checked with his office, received Leslie's message, and immediately hurried to the hospital.

"Why don't you go on in?" Dr. Poston urged.

Leslie, Abby with her, opened the door into the hospital corridor just as Hugh reached her room. "Hugh!"

"Thank God you're all right. For a while I thought I was going to greet my son or daughter, but the doc tells me we're still going to have to wait awhile. Think your chauffeur would object if I escorted you home?"

Abby patted his arm. "Of course, I wouldn't. I'll just be running along and you two can handle getting her released. Don't stop for dinner, either, I'll bring you kids something over."

"I'm sorry you had to go through the ordeal alone," Hugh said later that evening when he and Leslie were sitting outside with Fritz. Although still officially winter, the day was pleasantly warm, more like late spring or early summer.

"You've apologized about twenty times, Hugh. I

thought I'd made it clear everything's okay." Which wasn't entirely accurate, but he seemed to be suffering so, Leslie couldn't find it in herself to berate him over his absence.

"Considering our conversation last night," he kept on, "I suppose I find that difficult to accept."

"Accept it," she ordered. "We both said things yesterday that were best left unsaid. Certainly, I—" A muscle cramp seized Leslie's calf, interrupting her. She grimaced, then bent down to massage the leg.

Hugh immediately took over the massage, his tender ministrations making Leslie want to reassure him further. "It wasn't my intention to criticize you last night," she said. "It just came out all wrong. What I meant to say was that I miss you but I hated to see you tiring yourself out traipsing back and forth between Dallas and Houston all week because of me. I started out trying to be sympathetic."

"And got your head bitten off in return?"

She nodded, then smiled. "You shouldn't jump to conclusions. I'm doing my best not to."

"Care to explain that last statement?"

Leslie hesitated, wondering exactly how to say this. "Part of me…part of me could—" She paused and started anew. "Oh, I suppose what I'm trying to say is that I understand what's prompted all this attention from you and I won't let it go to my head."

"And to what exactly are you attributing the attention?"

"I realize it's for the baby, not really for me. Regardless, I want you to know it's appreciated, but unnecessary. I'm perfectly capable of taking care of the baby—and of myself."

"As you've so dramatically proven over the

years.'' He got up and walked over to the edge of the
patio, staring out into the expanse of dark yard.

''So we're back to sniping,'' Leslie said, pulling
herself up from the lawn chair and pressing her fingers
into the small of her back trying to relieve some of
the discomfort caused by her disproportionate weight.
''On that note, I think I'll head for bed.''

He didn't try to stop her.

Less than thirty minutes had passed and Leslie was in
bed reading a manual about baby's first year when her
door opened. ''You could have knocked,'' she said,
laying the book aside.

Hugh didn't respond, but simply walked over and
yanked off the covers, then picked her up. ''What are
you doing?'' she demanded, pushing a hand against
his chest in protest.

''Something I should have done months ago,'' he
said, carrying her into the master bedroom. He let
Leslie gently slide to the floor as he pulled the
comforter down, then picked her up again and depos-
ited her in the bed.

''I'm too heavy for you to lift,'' Leslie said belat-
edly. *What is happening here?*

He didn't argue, but bent to kiss her, long and lovingly. After the kiss, he reached down to pat her
rounded stomach through the cotton gown she wore.
The baby inside responded with a series of kicks, as
though protecting its territory.

Hugh looked up quizzically. ''Does that hurt?'' he
asked. He was making circles with his hand, touching
her stomach all over in fascination.

''No, it doesn't really hurt,'' she said. ''Only a bit
uncomfortable when he's kicking like a football
punter, but still, the sensation isn't painful.'' *Like this*

closeness is right now. She wanted so much to grasp his hand and hold on to it for dear life, to ensure they were never apart again.

"You said 'he.' Do you want a boy?" he asked, sitting on the edge of the bed, his ear now against her stomach.

Leslie had advised Hugh of her decision not to take advantage of technology to learn the child's sex in advance. A pang of remorse. It *should* have been a joint decision. "It doesn't really matter. As long as the baby's healthy. How about you? Would you prefer a boy?"

"Uh-uh," Hugh answered, sitting up and kissing her on the forehead. "I want a daughter who looks like her mother." He rose from the edge of the bed and started undressing, leaving Leslie only for a quick trip to the adjoining bath. When he returned, in pajama bottoms, he clicked off the lamp on the bedside table and crawled in beside her. He smelled of soap and toothpaste.

This scene made no sense to Leslie and she lay still, frozen in place, waiting for Hugh to make the first move.

He eased an arm under her shoulder and pulled her closer, so her hair draped across his chest. Leslie tensed. "Is being in my arms so distasteful?" he said, without releasing his hold.

"Surprising," Leslie answered truthfully, "but not at all distasteful."

"I've wanted you here since that first day you moved back, you know."

"Actually I didn't. The welcome mat hasn't exactly been laid out."

He put a finger against her lips. "Don't start," he said. "All we're going to do is talk, quietly and without rancor. Something we should have done long, long before now. Tell me what you're thinking, Les. Tell me about your needs, your fears...."

She sighed. After all that had happened, could Hugh finally be ready to listen? "Are you really interested?"

"Try me."

"I feared losing myself in you," she said honestly, "the way I did before. Subverting my goals, my ambitions, to pursue yours." *Now I fear losing you*, she added silently.

"Which goals do you mean?" Hugh's voice was calm, without any hint of belligerence.

"Seeing more of the world than Texas. Using my language skills in their native setting. Before we met, I had applied for a foreign study scholarship."

"And what happened to it?"

"By the time it was approved we were planning to marry so I turned it down."

"You never told me."

"The law firms were recruiting you hot and heavy. I didn't want you to miss your chance."

"So you missed yours. And nursed a grudge over it?"

The question wasn't asked angrily and Leslie had no problem replying. "Maybe a little. Funny how unimportant it seems now. I'm sorry."

"I'm the one who should be sorry—again. I saddled you with my ambitions, caused you to take jobs you didn't like—"

"I've never said that."

"No, but I figured it out on my own. You jumped from job to job before you signed on at Byers Textiles. Obviously something was wrong. But I just thought at the time that you needed to find the right position. And to grow up a bit.''

''You weren't all wrong. There was both job dissatisfaction and immaturity. Even though the nine-to-five grind is not my thing, I do like working with Bert. I've settled in there quite nicely.''

''I also saddled you with a house, and now there's the baby.''

''I *want* our baby,'' she answered his unspoken question.

''So do I, Les. But I also want *us* too—really back together, not just sharing a house, but sharing a life. The way we should be. Surely, somehow, we can manage that and still both have our dreams, pursue our careers.''

''The only career that matters to me now is wife and mother.''

''What about seeing the world?''

''You and the baby *are* my world. I don't plan to set foot out of Dallas unless it's with you.''

''Do you want to return to Byers?''

''As a free-lancer perhaps, or back to a couple of days a week. Our family comes first.'' Leslie was silent for a moment. She didn't want to bring up an old argument, but she needed reassurance from Hugh. ''What about your work obligations?'' She held her breath waiting for his answer.

''Nothing for you to worry about now.'' He brushed his lips across hers. ''You need to get some sleep.''

Leslie knew Hugh hadn't answered her question. Nevertheless, wrapped cozily in his arms, she did fall asleep.

Leslie's moans awakened Hugh near dawn. ''Darling, what is it?'' he whispered. Her eyes were closed, but

Hugh doubted she was asleep. "Les,—" he took her hand, "—I'm here."

Her brown eyes opened. "You're really here?"

"Of course I am."

"But the trial...you were supposed to leave for Houston." Leslie's muddled mind told her she was hallucinating, that in reality Hugh was in that court-room in southeast Texas.

"No, *this* is where I'm supposed to be. Our family comes first with me, too, darling, and from now on I'll prove it to you. I'm going to request a continuance on the trial. If that won't work, then I'll see about getting someone else to step in for me. Big client or not, I don't want to leave home again until you and our baby can travel with me." He kissed her long and lovingly.

"I've almost gone crazy with missing you, Les. There's no way I'll miss our baby's arrival. I love you."

"You love me?" Leslie sat up in bed and gazed down at him.

"Of course, you silly goose." Hugh pulled her back into his arms. "I'll love you until my days on this earth are ended."

"I thought you stopped when—"

"I *never* stopped," he interrupted, easing Leslie to her side so as not to put undue pressure on their child.

"But I wanted you, I needed you. You just let me stay in France."

"I prayed every day that you'd come to your senses and return. I saw it as a test. You were the one who left so you had to be the one who— What a stupid oaf I was for not chasing after you, for letting ego rule over love."

"Then you really don't mind about the baby?"

Hugh laughed. "Mind? I was on cloud nine when I learned you were pregnant. The baby tied you to me, gave me some time to rekindle your love for me."

"You mean *your* love for me."

"No, dearest. That never wavered, although I didn't do a good job of letting you know. I should have told you constantly...showed you.... Please banish all those doubts of yours. Please trust me. I love you, Leslie Campbell."

"And I love you." Leslie didn't want an anguished groan to accent the words, but it came anyway. The labor pains had restarted, and this time she was positive it was no false alarm.

EPILOGUE

"This sort of 'honeymoon' wasn't exactly what you had in mind all those years you dreamed of Paris," Hugh said as he and Leslie strolled hand-in-hand through the gardens of Versailles.

"Not exactly," she admitted with a smile. "Not many couples bring a daughter and mother-in-law along." She glanced back to check the pair following them. Hugh's mother was pushing a stroller holding the giggling child. "But I just couldn't leave Vicki."

"You never can. That little girl's amassing enough frequent-flier miles to qualify for a flight around the world." The three of them had made several trips, some in connection with Hugh's work, other short jaunts just for fun.

"Did you mind Mother coming this time?"

"No. Like you said, we need a reliable baby-sitter for when we want to be alone. Thank goodness your mom's retired and doesn't mind helping out."

"Mind? She's in hog heaven. Not just seeing Paris but being with her grandchild. She thinks Victoria hung the moon."

"Smart woman."

"Uh-huh." Hugh ducked behind some shrubbery and drew Leslie into his arms for a kiss.

"Sure smooching is allowed here?" she whispered, her lips nuzzling his neck.

"Well, we're in France after all. The land of lovers. It's not just allowed, it's expected." He gazed into her eyes. "Les, I...I wish we'd made this trip two years ago. That I'd—"

She placed her fingertips across his lips, silencing the words. "No recriminations, remember? Our marriage, our love, is stronger now because of all that happened."

"You're right," he agreed, stealing a second kiss before pulling her back onto the path. "I'm glad Vicki's like you, though. Look." He pointed toward the child who was fingering a crimson-flowered bush. "She's already learning how important it is to smell the roses."

They both rushed over when the little girl let out a whimper and held up a tiny pricked finger which was promptly kissed by all three adults. "She's also learning roses have thorns," Leslie said ruefully, as they watched Hugh's mother distract Vicki by pushing her to another colorful bed of flowers. "It took me much too long to realize that life has two sides."

"But we've hit the right balance now, haven't we, darling? Neither too much work—"

"Nor too much play," Leslie finished the sentence. "Yes, dearest, we've found the perfect balance. I'm glad you didn't give up on me."

"And I say a daily prayer of thankfulness that you came back home. I love you, I love what our marriage has become, I love our daughter. I'm not sure I even understood the meaning of the word before," Hugh admitted.

"I won't let you forget it again," Leslie promised. "Now don't you think it's time we got back to the hotel? Vicki's ready for a nap." Taking Hugh's hand again, Leslie added challengingly, "Maybe we should take one, too."

"A nap?" His expression was innocent.

"Or something."

"I think I prefer 'or something,'" Hugh replied with a grin.

4 FREE

books and a surprise gift!

We would like to take this opportunity to thank you for reading this Mills & Boon® book by offering you the chance to take FOUR more specially selected titles from the Enchanted™ series absolutely FREE! We're also making this offer to introduce you to the benefits of the Reader Service™—

★ FREE home delivery
★ FREE gifts and competitions
★ FREE monthly newsletter
★ Books available before they're in the shops
★ Exclusive Reader Service discounts

Accepting these FREE books and gift places you under no obligation to buy, you may cancel at any time, even after receiving your free shipment. Simply complete your details below and return the entire page to the address below. *You don't even need a stamp!*

YES! Please send me 4 free Enchanted books and a surprise gift. I understand that unless you hear from me, I will receive 6 superb new titles every month for just £2.30 each, postage and packing free. I am under no obligation to purchase any books and may cancel my subscription at any time. The free books and gift will be mine to keep in any case.

N8XE

Ms/Mrs/Miss/Mr..................................Initials ....
                                                            BLOCK CAPITALS PLEASE
Surname ....

Address ....

....

....Postcode....................................

Send this whole page to:
THE READER SERVICE, FREEPOST, CROYDON, CR9 3WZ
(Eire readers please send coupon to: P.O. BOX 4546, DUBLIN 24.)

MILLS & BOON®

Next Month's Romances

♡

Each month you can choose from a wide variety of romance novels from Mills & Boon®. Below are the new titles to look out for next month from the Presents™ and Enchanted™ series.

Presents™

SINFUL PLEASURES	Anne Mather
THE RELUCTANT HUSBAND	Lynne Graham
THE NANNY AFFAIR	Robyn Donald
RUNAWAY FIANCÉE	Sally Wentworth
THE BRIDE'S SECRET	Helen Brooks
TEMPORARY PARENTS	Sara Wood
CONTRACT WIFE	Kay Thorpe
RED-HOT LOVER	Sarah Holland

Enchanted™

AN IDEAL WIFE	Betty Neels
DASH TO THE ALTAR	Ruth Jean Dale
JUST ANOTHER MIRACLE!	Caroline Anderson
ELOPING WITH EMMY	Liz Fielding
THE WEDDING TRAP	Eva Rutland
LAST CHANCE MARRIAGE	Rosemary Gibson
MAX'S PROPOSAL	Jane Donnelly
LONE STAR LOVIN'	Debbie Macomber

On sale from 6th April 1998

H1 9803

Available at most branches of
WH Smith, John Menzies, Martins, Tesco,
Asda, Volume One, Sainsbury and Safeway

MILLS & BOON®

THREE BRIDES, NO GROOM

BY
DEBBIE MACOMBER

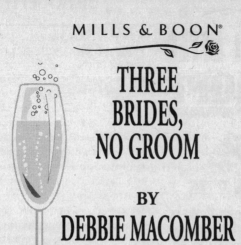

We are delighted to bring you three brand-new stories about love and marriage from one of our most popular authors.

Even though the caterers were booked, the bouquets bought and the bridal dresses were ready to wear...the grooms suddenly got cold feet. And that's when three women decided they weren't going to get mad...they were going to get even!

On sale from 6th April 1998
Price £5.25

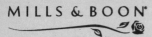
MILLS & BOON®

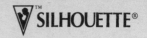
SILHOUETTE®

SPECIAL OFFER
£5 OFF

FLYING FLOWERS

Beautiful fresh flowers, sent by 1st class post to any UK and Eire address.

We have teamed up with Flying Flowers, the UK's premier 'flowers by post' company, to offer you £5 off a choice of their two most popular bouquets the 18 mix (CAS) of 10 multihead and 8 luxury bloom Carnations and the 25 mix (CFG) of 15 luxury bloom Carnations, 10 Freesias and Gypsophila. All bouquets contain fresh flowers 'in bud', added greenery, bouquet wrap, flower food, care instructions, and personal message card. They are boxed, gift wrapped and sent by 1st class post.

To redeem £5 off a Flying Flowers bouquet, simply complete the application form below and send it with your cheque or postal order to; **HMB Flying Flowers Offer, The Jersey Flower Centre, Jersey JE1 5FF.**

ORDER FORM (Block capitals please) Valid for delivery anytime until 30th November 1998 MAB/0298/A

Title ....Initials ....Surname ....

Address..

....

....Postcode ....

Signature...Are you a Reader Service Subscriber **YES/NO**

Bouquet(s)**18 CAS** (Usual Price £14.99) **£9.99** ☐ **25 CFG** (Usual Price £19.99) **£14.99** ☐

I enclose a cheque/postal order payable to Flying Flowers for £.............................or payment by

VISA/MASTERCARD ☐☐☐☐☐☐☐☐☐☐☐☐☐☐☐☐ Expiry Date.........../.........../...........

PLEASE SEND MY BOUQUET TO ARRIVE BY.........../.........../.........

TO Title ....Initials ....Surname ....

Address..

....

....Postcode ....

Message (Max 10 Words) ....

....

Please allow a minimum of four working days between receipt of order and 'required by date' for delivery.

You may be mailed with offers from other reputable companies as a result of this application. Please tick box if you would prefer not to receive such offers. ☐

Terms and Conditions Although dispatched by 1st class post to arrive by the required date the exact day of delivery cannot be guaranteed. Valid for delivery anytime until 30th November 1998. Maximum of 5 redemptions per household, photocopies of the voucher will be accepted.